"I've Never Forced A Woman In My Life, Jade,"

Reed told her. "I don't plan to start now."

He towered over her. His sheer bigness simultaneously served as an invitation and a warning. Jade unconsciously pressed her hands to her sides. "Reed, I'm not accusing you of force."

"Then what are you implying?"

"There's just no place in my life for a relationship."

"You're lying, but if that's how you want to play this out, fine."

"I'm not playing or lying."

"Aren't you?" He took a step closer.

"I've already told you that macho doesn't do a thing for me," she flared.

"Don't lie, Jade." His voice, already rough and low, went a full tone deeper. "I want you. I want you naked and in my bed. I want you any way I can have you, but that doesn't mean I won't respect your wishes."

Dear Reader:

Welcome to Silhouette Desire—sensual, compelling, believable love stories written by and for today's woman. When you open the pages of a Silhouette Desire, you open yourself up to a whole new world— a world of promising passion and endless love.

Each and every Silhouette Desire is a wonderful love story that is both sensuous *and* emotional. You're with the hero and heroine each and every step of the way—from their first meeting, to their first kiss ... to their happy ending. You'll experience all the deep joys—and occasional tribulations—of falling in love.

In future months, look for Silhouette Desire novels from some of your favorite authors, such as Naomi Horton, Nancy Martin, Linda Lael Miller and Lass Small, just to name a few.

So go wild with Desire. You'll be glad you did!

Lucia Macro
Senior Editor

LAURA TAYLOR

JADE'S PASSION

SILHOUETTE *Desire*

Published by Silhouette Books New York

America's Publisher of Contemporary Romance

SILHOUETTE BOOKS
300 East 42nd St., New York, N.Y. 10017

ISBN: 0-373-05586-2

First Silhouette Books printing August 1990

LAURA TAYLOR

views life as a potpourri of drama, humor and fantasy. After growing up in a career Air Force family, she acquired a degree in criminology and married her real-life "Top Gun" hero, a former Marine Corps aviator who shares her passion for both travel and their new life-style in the southern Ozarks of Arkansas. She was named as one of 1988's best new series writers for her first Silhouette Desire, *Troubled Waters*, then went on to make the romance bestseller list with *Wildflower*, her second Silhouette Desire. She has also won awards and accolades for her mainstream writing.

To Kathleen Creighton,
dear friend and valued peer.
With special thanks
for the inspiration for this book.
and
To the Gold Coast Chapter of RWA—
my home team via
the U.S. Mail and Ma Bell.

One

Despite your obvious dedication to an after-school facility for the school-age children of homeless families living in San Diego's inner city, the Lindley Foundation has chosen another charity as our annual grant recipient, Miss Howell.''

The caller paused. Jade gripped the telephone and mentally scrambled to regain her emotional equilibrium, but shock and disappointment prevented her from filling in the empty seconds.

"The director seriously doubts the long-term viability of the Activity Center," the woman continued. "However, if the center is still operational next year, perhaps you'll wish to reapply for funding at that time. Miss Howell, both the Lindley family and the foundation staff wish you every success with this endeavor, and we also hope you understand that our decision in no way reflects negatively on your ability."

The formal tone of the caller and the content of her message resembled a death knell. Jade surprised herself and managed the standard amenities required to conclude their conversation. She also fought her inclination to shout her frustration at the unfairness of the Lindley Foundation's decision; she knew such behavior would be self-indulgent and completely out of character.

She lightly rested her trembling hand on the receiver for several seconds even after she eased it into the cradle of the phone. Think, she ordered herself. Think! There had to be another way to get the money.

She covered her face with her hands and exhaled heavily. Despair flirted with her consciousness, but she resisted the negative emotion. Straightening, she nervously finger-combed her bangs and the shoulder-length fall of dark brown hair that framed her face, before pressing her fingertips to the aching muscles of her neck.

As she worked the knots of tension from her nape, she realized that she couldn't let herself risk even the slightest thought of failure. Too much was at stake: eighteen months of effort on her part, and the well-being of countless children.

She'd fought too long and too hard to make the Activity Center a reality to throw in the towel now. Dropping her hands to her sides, she stiffened her spine. The Lindley Foundation might not believe in the viability of the center, but she did. Even more important, the children believed in her. She silently renewed her vow not to disappoint them.

Wandering out of her office—a converted storeroom that contained a scarred oak desk, a chair and a secondhand file cabinet—Jade ransacked her mind for an alternative source of funding that would allow her to make the final payment for the renovations presently being made to the once abandoned warehouse. She'd foolishly allowed herself to count on the foundation's grant money, primarily because of the confidence and enthusiasm the Lindley family had expressed concerning her plans during a fund-raiser they'd held for the center a few months prior to the start of the renovation work.

Jade couldn't stop her shoulders from slumping, nor could she eliminate the bleak expression on her face as she walked down a long hallway and into the cavernous warehouse. Emotional fatigue battled with her stubborn nature, briefly triumphing as she stepped into the controlled chaos of the construction area.

Accustomed now to the ongoing din created by high-pressure jackhammers, power saws and the loud voices of more than two dozen workers, Jade didn't pay attention to the shouting around her as she unwittingly stepped into the path of a forklift carrying an enormous load of ceiling beams.

Reed Townsend mopped the sweat from his face with the bandanna he normally kept knotted across his forehead. The heat—intense for August in San Diego—took its toll on even the sturdiest construction worker, and he was no exception. He glanced around the gutted warehouse as he re-tied the bandanna.

In his mind's eye, he could already see the end result of the rehab project his company had been hired to do. Instead of having to cope with the dangers of inner-city neighborhoods, the children of homeless families attracted to the mild Southern California climate would have a safe place to play by mid-September.

The Activity Center would also provide a respite from the realities of cast-off clothing, poor nutrition and nights spent in public shelters or in abandoned vehicles on unsafe streets. Equally satisfying was his realization that he had been able to combine business with his own private humanitarian interests when he'd accepted the job from the prickly director of the Activity Center.

Just the thought of Jade Howell brought a blunt word of frustration to his lips. And his thoughts of her, like his nights, tortured him until he could force her from his mind and refocus on the activity around him.

The near-deafening roar created by men and machinery that permeated the warehouse invaded his consciousness and soothed him. This was his arena; and excellence in all things was his personal credo. His pursuit of the latter hadn't changed since he'd fled the heavy fists of his drunkard father at the age of seventeen. Now thirty-five, he retained his high standards. He expected they always would.

He knew people would think him odd if he admitted that what they considered irritating construction noise often reminded him of a concisely orchestrated musical score. He also decided that there was something almost erotic about this kind of sensory assault, perhaps because the intensity and the energy of his surroundings brought to mind an almost forgotten memory of a past lover who had always insisted on playing the *1812 Overture* whenever they had sex.

The sensual image in his mind coerced a reluctant smile from him, but the slight softening of his hard-featured face vanished almost immediately when he heard a shouted warning. Its discordant tone signified alarm and prophesied impending disaster.

Reed quickly scanned the warehouse. His heart tripped to a halt in his chest when he spotted Jade. He knew that the forklift driver couldn't see her because her slight frame and khaki clothing made her presence undetectable in the shadowy areas at the perimeter of the warehouse. The precariously balanced beams further obscured the driver's visibility.

Cursing loudly, Reed sprinted across the sawdust-littered cement and around clusters of workers involved in a variety of tasks before leaping over a series of low stacks of lumber. His long-legged stride propelled him toward Jade and the forklift lumbering in her direction.

Every second counted.

He'd warned Jade to stay out of the construction area and until today, she had sporadically heeded his orders. Grabbing her from behind, he spun her around and slammed her against his chest as he moved them both out of harm's way.

Shock and outrage made her yelp. Stunningly intense physical awareness of a powerful male body made her cringe. Breathlessness, brought on by his swift seizure, kept her from demanding release.

She struggled as he hauled her, thrown over his broad shoulder like a sack of potatoes, down the hallway and into her office. Her efforts to free herself proved useless, though. And his body heat and the unleashed power of his hold vaulted her already reeling senses into orbit.

Reed worked at regaining his self-control. His heart pumped fiercely at the thought of what could have happened to her, and his breathing, already ragged, stopped altogether for a brief moment when his mind produced a battered image of this delicate woman.

Jade squirmed, still trying to dislodge herself from his shoulder. Her movement and her flailing fists finally penetrated his mind, momentarily displacing the word *delicate* and substituting ones like *stubborn*, *combative* and *obstinate*. Reed lowered her to the floor, but not before he let her compact body slide the length of his tensely muscled anatomy. Only then did he allow her to regain her footing.

Although furious with her for her carelessness, as well as with himself for prolonging the agony of having her in his arms, he still didn't completely release her. Instead, he gripped her slender shoulders tightly, his fingertips burning as he held her in place, his face taut with tension.

Somewhere in the back of his mind was the realization that he'd wanted this woman with an escalating hunger for the entire eight weeks that they'd known each other. But now he craved her with the reckless kind of desire he'd long ago consigned to the hot-blooded days of his youth.

"What do you think you're doing?" she demanded.

Intimidating in both manner and appearance, thanks to his size and harsh expression, Reed continued to seethe. Words eluded him. He felt heat gust up inside him with the stunning force of a punch to the gut. The blow threatened the self-control that had always been a part of his personality.

Jade flinched when she noticed his expression, but she refused to look away. She was paying the freight around here, damn it! How dare the man behave as though her warehouse had suddenly become his personal playground? And how dare he embarrass and humiliate her in front of his crew?

Shoving aside the dense curtain of hair that had fallen across her cheek, she glared at him. Her eyes, already a rich dark brown, went a full shade darker to black as fury mounted within her.

Reed reacted to the mutinous look on her face and the anger glittering in her eyes, but not before wondering why in hell she was glaring at him like some outraged virgin in a grade-B Western.

"What did you think you were doing out there, lady? Taking a casual stroll in a park?"

Her emotions already tattered, she jerked free of him and returned his surly look. It had already taken every bit of her determination to ignore the disabling heat that had flowed through her when he'd carried her, slid her down his body and then held her in place in front of him as they'd taken each other's measure.

"Mr. Townsend, don't yell at me. I won't have it!"

Reed swore, loudly and eloquently.

Jade felt her nerves start to sizzle, and she ground her teeth. Stunned by his thunderous expression, she concluded that he'd somehow turned into a madman. How in the world, she wondered, could she ever have found him attractive? And why had he tackled her in the warehouse?

Reed—concern and suppressed fury still roaring through him—swore again. With his denim-encased legs spread wide and his muscled chest straining the seams of his knit pullover, he looked intent on and fully capable of a violent act.

Alarmed, Jade stepped back. Not knowing what to make of him, she retreated in the general direction of her desk.

Until now, he'd simply been brash, bold, overbearing, outspoken, self-assured and demanding. He looked like a gladiator, but he often behaved like a temperamental dictator.

In short, he was everything she actively avoided in a man. He was also everything she secretly craved.

Jade nearly groaned aloud at that last startling realization. She ruthlessly countered it with the reminder that there was no room in her life for the vulnerability and dependence that accompanied male-female relationships. Her energy, her commitment and her passion would always be dedicated to the young people served by the Activity Center. They needed her.

Still, she experienced bewildering emotions every time Reed got within ten feet of her. She hated the uncertainty he always managed to inspire, and she hated it even more that he frightened her to the point of witlessness. Not physical fear, of course; just a sense of being in a constant emotional tailspin.

He made her hungry with need and alive with longing. He made her *want*, in the most primitive way a woman can want a man. For the past two months, Jade had fought every dark urge that had come to life inside her. She couldn't stop fighting now. She hurriedly put the brakes on her racing thoughts and reckless hormones. No man on the planet was worth the loss of her self-control.

Her mental tug-of-war complete for the moment, she said the first thing that popped into her mind. "Keep your hands to yourself, Mr. Townsend. I won't be manhandled or mauled by the likes of you. Is that perfectly clear? Or do I need to reduce this conversation to caveman grunts?"

Reed exploded, unleashing an avalanche of tension. "You almost got yourself killed, you self-righteous little fool!"

"I did no such thing!" she shouted back.

"I told you to stay the hell out of the warehouse."

"I don't take orders from you, Mr. Townsend. You work for me. Or have you managed to forget that little fact?"

"Lady," he ground out, "I work for myself. I may hire out my services and the services of Foothills Construction, but I make the rules. I made the rules two months ago, but you've consistently ignored them whenever it suited you."

"I have not! What I have done, however, is accommodate this dictatorship you've created. At least be honest about that much."

"You haven't accommodated me in the one way that would really count, Jade Howell."

His voice was low, hoarse and shockingly intense, but Jade didn't miss one word of what he'd just said. Or its implication. She gaped at him before finding her voice. "What did you just say?"

"You heard me." He jerked free the red bandanna that served as a headband and wound it around his fist.

Jade looked first at him and then at the twisting flash of red fabric with fascinated horror. She went from shock to fury in a flash.

Reed shook his head in disgust when he realized what he'd admitted. His loss of control rekindled his anger. He cursed her, then he cursed himself, in total silence. Not even his worst moments in combat during his Marine Corps days had been like this.

"Mr. Townsend—" she began.

He interrupted her. "Do you want me to pull my crews and let you tackle this place yourself?"

"You wouldn't dare!"

Reed moved toward her, his powerful physique as menacing as his current state of mind. "Watch me!"

She didn't budge, but the difference in their physical sizes made her quiver. "Don't threaten me, Mr. Townsend. We have a signed contract, and I expect you to honor it." *Even though God only knows how I'll be able to make the final payment.* She paled, certain that he could see her guilt.

They simply looked at each other then, the silence between them almost as earsplitting as the din in the construction area.

Reed used the silence to bring himself under control. In the soberest tone of voice Jade had ever heard him use, he finally said, "I grabbed you because you were in the path of a forklift carrying a load of ceiling beams. You didn't see the forklift, and the operator obviously couldn't see you because of where you were standing. If he'd hit you, there would have been little point in even calling an ambulance."

Jade blanched and grabbed the edge of the desk for support. Given the events of the past thirty minutes, it wasn't surprising that she felt as though someone had just tried to level her with a right hook. At least that's what she told herself when Reed surged forward and pulled her into his arms.

She stared up at him, momentarily dazed by the array of emotions in his dark eyes. She registered the gentleness of his embrace and how wonderfully protective his arms felt as he eased her against his chest.

And, for just the briefest of moments, she let herself need him, let herself accept her own vulnerability and her desire to depend on someone else's strength. Sighing, she rested her forehead on his chest and closed her eyes, promising herself that this little lapse of common sense would only last a few fortifying moments.

Needing him any longer than that would be a mistake. Needing anyone was a mistake. Need, she knew from bitter personal experience, invariably resulted in denial or outright abandonment. She could do without a refresher course on that little reality.

Reed knew he had to end the torture of her closeness soon or risk losing all control. He wanted her, of course; but not here, and not like this. But deep in his gut was the conviction that there would probably never be another time. They were too different; and bridging the wide gap that separated them didn't seem even remotely possible.

"Jade?"

"Yes?" She lifted her head and looked up. The confusion she felt was evident in her eyes.

"Are you all right?"

She nodded absently, her gaze riveted on his blunt-featured face. He sounded so caring, even with that rough voice of his. Bewildered and bemused, she couldn't stop staring at him.

His short sun-bleached hair, those dramatic slashing brows, his eyes, penetrating and the darkest blue she'd ever seen, a proud but slightly dented nose, cheekbones that made her think of Yosemite's El Capitan and mountain climbers, and a mouth that hinted at seduction even when he wasn't smiling, were already etched into her consciousness. As was his body—all six feet and however many complementary inches, tacked on for good measure, which gave new meaning to the words *masculine prowess*.

Reed Townsend was mature and male and in his prime, with strength and muscle and sinew honed to perfection by daily physical labor, and packaged in such a compelling manner as to be dangerous to all womankind.

"Jade?"

She blinked, nearly drowning in the steam generated by her unruly thoughts.

The sight of her flushed features, her huge brown eyes so wide and so achingly and unexpectedly vulnerable, and her soft bow-shaped lips, maddening and inviting by their very design, short-circuited his common sense.

Reed abandoned all his good intentions. He lowered his mouth and took her lips, his seductive gentleness in stark contrast to his rough exterior.

Jade stiffened with shock, but she couldn't hold out against Reed's incredible tenderness or the emotional tumult shattering her composure.

She simply succumbed to the madness of the moment.

Somewhere, perhaps in the farthest reaches of her mind, was the knowledge that this space in time had somehow been preordained by fate. The pragmatist residing nearby accused her of complete insanity.

Still, she allowed herself to be swept away by her own stunned emotions and the heart-stoppingly seductive play of Reed's intimate exploration. The sweep of his tongue softened her lips and the mobile movement of his mouth vanquished her emotions, holding her in thrall and suspending her in a sensory state that shook her to her soul.

The possessiveness of his hands as he molded her against his chest brought a gasp of disbelief to her lips. Reed trembled and thrust his tongue into her mouth, his embrace tightening when he felt Jade's acceptance of this intimacy.

Possession graduated to reckless desire. Jade felt the change in him. She also felt the swelling heat within herself. Raising her arms, she let her fingers, now bold and greedy, join at the base of his neck. She felt driven by some hot, dark force. Stunned, she could do nothing less than follow his lead, even if he took her straight into hell, which she sensed he could easily do.

He edged one hip against her desk and pulled her closer. When she didn't resist but pressed herself more fully against him, he forgot every cautionary word he'd ever muttered to himself about wanting an unattainable woman like Jade Howell—a woman so far beyond his reach that he knew he tested the limits of his own sanity by being anywhere near her.

Jade shuddered, responding to both Reed and the hot coil of desire winding tighter and tighter in her body. Need, heavy and throbbing deep inside her, and fear, so disabling that she sagged weakly in Reed's arms, collided within the confines of her scrambled mind.

He savored her. He devoured her. He couldn't believe she was actually in his arms, clinging to him, responding to him, wanting him. He hated the thought that this mindless torment might end, but he knew it would.

Despite her confusion, Jade sensed that she was on the brink of total capitulation. Alarm burst to life inside her, and she responded to it instinctively. She moaned, the small sound of resistance belying the need suffusing her senses.

Reed reacted immediately. It wasn't in him to force a woman to his will, no matter his hunger, no matter his driving desire for possession. Although his body throbbed painfully for want of her, he lifted his mouth from her lips and with a shaking hand, pressed her cheek to his shoulder.

He couldn't release her just yet, not with the combined tremors of need and restraint still shuddering through him. He needed her for just a few minutes more—minutes that might not appease his hunger, but minutes during which he would regain his shattered control, minutes during which he could try to prepare himself for her fury.

He also sensed that she might need time, too. Time to pull herself back together, time to rearm herself, time to restore herself to the image of the one-woman army. It was a role she seemed determined to play. That much he'd figured out in eight weeks.

Too shocked to even consider voicing her tangled emotions, Jade hid in the shelter of Reed's arms. How could she have let this happen? *Why* had she let this happen?

Rational thought evaded her. She didn't think of destiny or chemistry or the volatility of two opposing forces. Neither did she consider the very real possibility that they might not be natural adversaries. She'd considered the adversarial die cast between them during their first meeting and perpetuated each time they came into contact with each other.

Jade finally opened her eyes. What she saw unnerved her, and she tried to jerk free of Reed. He responded instantly to the change in her.

Turning, he noted their audience—one of his employees—with a grim expression and quickly shoved her behind him when the worker made no move to leave. Reed rebuked him, tersely and effectively. As Jade left the protection of Reed's body and crossed the room, she could hear the retreating footsteps of the man who had viewed at least a part of her loss of sanity.

"I . . . you . . . I mean, we shouldn't—"

He raised a hand, his eyes straying briefly to the two framed pieces of parchment hanging on the wall behind Jade. "Don't. I know what you're going to say."

"Do you?"

Her soft voice gnawed at his soul, but he remained expressionless, his fists clenched at his sides. "What just happened between us couldn't have been avoided much longer."

"You're wrong," she protested.

"I don't think so."

"It doesn't matter. It won't happen again."

Her self-contained tone startled him. He watched her tug at the hem of her blouse and smooth her ruffled bangs back into place. She seemed disconnected from everything that had just taken place. Puzzled, he watched her, noting her look of efficiency and cool disinterest.

Only Jade knew the cost of this studied indifference. When it became clear to her that Reed didn't plan to make the situation easy for either one of them, she walked around him, flinching slightly when he grabbed her wrist to halt her retreat.

She glanced at his hand before meeting his probing gaze. "Macho doesn't work for me, Mr. Townsend. Neither does your blunt brand of sexuality. I'm certain there are legions of beach bunnies just dying to accommodate you. Please let them."

Reed released her as though scalded. He didn't need to be reminded of how different they were. He already knew the facts, just as he knew that there was damn little he could do about them—at least not in this lifetime.

Dark eyes even narrower and more penetrating than usual, he demanded in a hard voice, "Be honest with yourself. Macho turns you on, doesn't it, *Ms.* Howell?"

Jade opened her mouth and then snapped it shut. She couldn't deny the obvious forever. *He* turned her on.

She simply stared at him, aware that she should thank him. Not for trying to seduce her, but for saving her life. The words hovered on the tip of her tongue. Pure stubbornness kept her from uttering them just yet. Being in this man's debt capped off a truly horrendous morning.

He smiled at her then—a knowing, macho smile that drove a shiver up her spine and made her furious, with him and with herself. Jade wanted to smack him. Heavens! She longed to smack him almost as much as she'd longed for the satisfaction of ice cream on a hot summer day as a child. She clenched her fists, but her palms still itched unmercifully.

"Thank you for saving me from being run down by the forklift, Mr. Townsend," she said in an even tone that implied he could now take a fast jog to hell, for all she cared.

"You're welcome, Ms. Howell."

She settled into her chair, her gaze fixed on the fund-raising folder on her desk. This madness had to stop. She had calls to make. Calls that might help her pay this man's bill.

Reed remained slouched against the desk. He watched her, amusement in his eyes and a deep ache in his soul. So prickly. So sexy. So stubborn. Jade Howell was all that and more. It was the *more* he wanted to discover. Having sampled her arousal, he wanted the banquet implicit in her smoldering passion.

Jade wondered what she would have to do to get him to leave. He couldn't remain in her office indefinitely. And she couldn't withstand forever the impulse that urged her to walk right back into his arms.

"Can I help you, Mr. Townsend?"

"Honey," he drawled, certain the sarcastic endearment would unsettle her, "you could help me straight into heaven if you wanted to."

She snapped the pencil she held into two perfectly even pieces. Taking a deep breath, she lifted her gaze to his face. "I'm busy. I trust you are, too."

He grinned, but his amused expression soon disappeared. Hot and cold. Fire and ice. The woman was one hell of an actress. He'd never known anyone, man or woman, who could undergo such abrupt mood and behavior changes so quickly, so effortlessly. But something nagged at him. The skill seemed too refined, too instinctive. What kind of life had she lived that would require the walls she repeatedly erected around herself?

"Have dinner with me."

"No...thank you."

"Another time?" he asked as he straightened.

She pressed her palms to the folder in front of her when she noticed that her hands were shaking. The fury within her fizzled out like a doused firecracker. Only numbness remained. She was oddly grateful, because the alternative entailed emotions too alarming to consider at the moment.

"Mr. Townsend, please go back to work," she whispered. "I don't have the energy to engage in a battle of wits with you right now."

Startled, Reed hesitated. Fire and ice had just given way to surprising vulnerability. He stepped away from her desk, considering his options as he walked to the door.

"How about a truce? Call me Reed, and I won't try to talk you into going out with me again for at least twenty-four hours," he teased, the expression on his face almost boyish.

She nodded faintly before he sauntered out of her office, his long-legged stride enhancing the powerful muscles in his thighs, his narrow hips and the remarkable width of his shoulders.

A tear slid down her cheek. Another followed, and one swiftly after that. Jade eased her head back, closed her eyes and began to pray for a miracle for herself and for the center.

Two

Jade needed a new chair. Along with about fifty thousand other things! She exhaled softly, shifted in the badly sprung relic she'd purchased at a used-furniture store more than a year ago, and then glanced at her watch. Nearly midnight. She also needed sleep.

Studying the instruction booklet in front of her, she continued to cross-check the thirty-page federal grant application she'd been working on for the past five hours. With luck, she would be able to drop the forms at the main post office on her way home.

After a day of rattled nerves and self-doubt, courtesy of Reed Townsend and the Lindley Foundation, she'd opted for take-out Chinese and for an evening of paperwork in her office at the deserted center. She felt less unsure of herself now, although Reed Townsend was never far from her thoughts.

When the phone rang, Jade reached for it without looking up. "Activity Center. How may I help you?"

The caller gripped the phone, the knuckles of his hand turning white. Tension streamed through his taut body, but he made himself speak in a softly measured tone as he held a length of fabric over the receiver to disguise his voice.

"Jade Howell?"

"Yes."

Reed experienced a clash of conflicting emotions. Frustration with Jade for working alone in the warehouse late at night, the pure pleasure he found in the sound of her voice and deep regret that he couldn't identify himself. The latter was a long-standing rule, one he never violated. None of the charities that benefited from his generous nature knew his identity. They never would.

Jade, in particular, could never know.

Charity given was sufficient reward, he reminded himself. Besides, he certainly didn't fit the refined image of a philanthropist, and he knew he never would.

Even more important, his personal code of honor and his sense of fair play flinched at the very thought of Jade feeling indebted to him, no matter how hungry he might be for her, no matter how frustrated he might become. And if today was any example, his desire for her would continue to thrive and his frustration would steadily mount.

Still, his pride warred with his hunger for this woman. A curse of pure self-reproach echoed in his skull and wrenched him back to reality.

Jade grew uncomfortable with the silence on the line. "Are you still there?"

"I'd like to ask you some questions about the center. Have you the time, Miss Howell?"

She leaned back in her chair, wincing when it squeaked in protest. "I do have the time, but may I ask your name before we begin?"

"I prefer to remain anonymous whenever I make a donation to a worthy cause. Is that condition acceptable to you?"

She pondered his reply and his question for a moment before responding. Despite limited experience with philanthropists, she knew some could be quite eccentric. If this person was a potential benefactor, she didn't want to deter his interest. Desperation and curiosity got the best of her.

"I'll accept your condition if you'll assure me that your interest in the center is sincere." By way of explanation, she added, "I've had several crank calls in recent months from people who have pledged donations, but who haven't followed up on their promises. Then, of course, there are the usual heavy breathers and an assortment of oddballs that could test the patience of a saint. I feel genuine sympathy for their shrinks."

Reed's anxiety for her safety intensified, making his tone curt. "I don't waste my time, Miss Howell. And my personal behavior has never been such that I've required the services of a psychiatrist."

His voice held the clear ring of truth and authority, but Jade felt no embarrassment at having asked for reassurance. She assumed that even serial killers could sound sincere!

"Thank you for clarifying the situation."

"Certainly. You're working rather late, aren't you?"

"There's a lot to do," she replied neutrally.

"Given the location of the center, is that wise?"

Why this concern with her working hours? Uneasiness crept into her voice, although she tried to tone it down as she spoke. "I'm really quite safe here. The doors are sturdy, and the locks are quite strong."

"Then I will assume they are secured."

He sounded so formal and so parental that she almost smiled. "Thank you for your concern, but there really isn't any need to worry."

"If you say so, Miss Howell."

"I'm not foolish enough to risk my own safety."

Reed recalled the forklift incident, but he didn't comment further on the subject. "I understand the renovations of the Activity Center are proceeding on schedule. Are you pleased with Foothills Construction?"

She added "well-informed" right below "authoritative" on her mental list of his personality attributes. "Certainly, but what's even more important is that the city building inspector is pleased."

"And Mr. Townsend?" he pressed, knowing he was treading in a minefield but unable to help himself. "Is he fulfilling his obligations to you?"

"Mr. Townsend is quite capable." Of driving her right out of her mind.

He heard the edge in her voice. "Am I making you uncomfortable?"

"No, of course not."

"Good."

"You said you wanted to hear about the center?"

"That's right." Reed reached for his glass of bourbon and took a quick sip. The fabric covering the receiver slipped and he repositioned it, but not before the surf crashed against the hard-packed sand less than fifteen feet from his deck.

Jade wondered at the odd sound, but she didn't say anything. "Would you like me to start at the beginning? I don't know what you've read in the newspapers about the center."

"I've been aware of the center for several months now. It's my understanding that you convinced the city of San Diego to donate an abandoned warehouse as a home for the Activity Center. I also understand that your purpose in making such a request was and is to limit the exposure to school-age homeless children to the less desirable elements who populate the inner-city streets."

"You're very well-informed."

"I always try to be." He paused for a moment and then observed, "You must be quite persuasive."

"Not really. I just believe in what I'm doing." She didn't mention her anxiety about achieving her goal, her fear of not having sufficient funding to ensure the continued operation of the center or her panic at the thought of not being able to pay Reed Townsend's final bill.

"Why?"

"Why what?"

"I'd like to understand your motivation."

She fell silent for a moment, uncertainty about how to proceed plaguing her. Her past had so much to do with her present. "Why do you really want to know?" she asked in a small voice.

"I don't ask questions unless I consider the answers important," he replied.

He couldn't tell her that he wanted to understand her. And in order to understand her, he had to have some grasp of what drove her. The Reed Townsend she knew, the man who wore a hard hat and work boots, who swore like the marine he'd once been, and who appeared to have the sensitivity of a man who ate nails for breakfast, certainly didn't fit the image of a confidant. Aware of her academic and professional background, he knew she would be more likely to seek out a peer. Hence he now relied on the old adage that

it was sometimes easier to talk to a stranger. He hoped she
would agree.

"You remind me of someone I know."

Reed straightened in alarm. "Is this person a friend?"

She chuckled softly. "I'm not sure."

"No relationship is ever perfect," he observed. "Most
take effort and understanding."

Jade softened. She felt her resistance to the thought of
talking to this stranger dissolve under the odd way he had of
expressing himself. She sensed kindness and compassion
behind his curiosity and his desire for privacy.

Perceiving continued reluctance on her part, Reed pressed
carefully. "Any information you wish to share will help me
make my final decision. And you can trust me to treat
whatever you say as a personal confidence."

She rarely shared her trust or her past with anyone. And
she wasn't even certain where or how to start. So she began
slowly, surprising herself when she was able to provide a
thumbnail sketch.

"My parents were killed in a car accident when I was four
years old. There was no one to take me in, so I grew up in
orphanages and foster homes in Los Angeles County. I suspect the reason I feel so strongly about providing alterna-
tives to the children of homeless families has to do with my
understanding of bureaucratic indifference and emotional
instability."

She continued by revealing an obscure fact documented
only in the closed file that L.A. County kept on her and
others like her. "I was moved ten times in less than fourteen years. The children the center serves are experiencing
the same kind of transiency, although for different reasons,
since most of them have at least one parent to depend on.
But if you factor in a social-services system that means well

but hasn't yet figured out how to deal with the homeless issue, the same problem keeps resurfacing: instability.''

"You can't be a mother to every child who walks in off the street."

"No, I can't," she readily agreed. "But I can provide an alternative to the streets. When we first opened the center, the volunteers and I all understood that we couldn't be substitute parents or provide a substitute home. Most of us are trained in either social work or education, so we're combining personal commitment and professional skills. And with the generosity of the public, we can offer a safe play area, toys and athletic equipment, field trips, special outings, a small library, adult supervision, counseling, and tutoring sessions for those who need help with schoolwork. We don't have all the answers, of course, but at least we're trying.''

"You operated the center for several months before the renovations began," Reed commented quietly.

"That's right, but once the building-safety inspector showed up, we knew we couldn't avoid the repairs the warehouse needed. Luckily we had enough money to initiate the renovation work."

"I assume you've temporarily relocated the children."

"The sisters at St. Matthew's offered their playground and classrooms until school starts again in September. Since they're just down the street from us, the children don't have transportation problems. I still administer the program and supervise the volunteers, even though most of my time is devoted to raising funds for the center."

"I assume you don't have children of your own."

"That's true, but how did you guess?"

"You're working late on a weeknight. Most parents would be home at this hour."

Was he chiding her again? "Perhaps," she agreed wistfully. She had little personal experience with a normal family relationship. "I think of the people at the center as my family."

"You're young yet. You have plenty of time for marriage and children," he observed. He wondered bleakly why he'd gone off on that tangent. He loathed thinking about Jade in the arms of another man.

"We'll see," she answered.

Sensing her reluctance to continue in this vein, Reed shifted the conversation back to the center.

"Is funding for the center consistent?"

"Not yet."

"Explain, please."

"I'm on a shoestring budget at present." She hesitated for a moment before admitting, "And funding I expected from a grant was denied."

"When?"

At that point Jade decided her caller was a lawyer. No one else would grill a person in quite this way. "This morning."

No wonder she'd behaved so erratically earlier in the day. "The Lindley Foundation?"

Startled, she asked, "How did you know?"

"The evening news, Miss Howell."

"Oh?"

"Anything the Lindley family does is considered newsworthy. In the case of their annual grant, they hold a press conference. The media always turns out because of the amount of money involved. I simply assumed that you had applied."

"You assumed correctly."

"You're very disappointed, Miss Howell."

Although he didn't ask but simply stated the obvious, she didn't acknowledge his comment one way or another. "Call me Jade, please. I think we've progressed beyond the need for formality.''

"Thank you.''

"Thank *you*,'' she said unexpectedly, some unnamed emotion rising up inside her.

"For what, Jade?''

"For caring enough about the center to call.'' She cleared her throat to rid it of the catch it had suddenly developed. "I was lonely tonight. It's nice to hear a friendly voice.''

His heart twisted painfully in his chest. Reed died a little inside, knowing that she would never have said such a thing had she known his true identity. "Didn't anyone ever tell you not to trust strangers?''

"I don't think I'm supposed to take candy from them, either,'' she quipped.

"I'm surprised by your frankness.''

"You shouldn't be. You're very easy to talk to.''

"You believe I'm trustworthy, then?''

"Yes.''

"I am,'' he stated firmly.

Jade added both "sincere'' and "shy'' to her list. "I concur.''

"Some people would consider you foolish.''

She smiled. "A lot of people already think I'm tilting at windmills.''

The train from Los Angeles selected that precise moment to whip through Reed's beachfront neighborhood, the train's engineer sounding a shrill whistle to announce his impending arrival at the Del Mar station. Reed clapped his hand over the receiver, cursing the unpredictable train schedule.

The sound startled Jade. "What was that?''

His action was too late, he realized, lowering his hand. "Nothing important.''

Jade shifted the puzzle pieces into place in her mind. Ocean sounds and train whistles translated into a waterfront location somewhere in the county, she decided. "You must live near the beach."

Reed ignored her observation. "What you're trying to accomplish at the Activity Center is admirable, but I can't help wondering why you seem so intent on handling everything yourself. I've heard no mention made of an administrative staff at the center in any of the information I've acquired. It appears that you're handling the administrative burden on your own. Is that wise?"

She immediately forgot about the train. "I've learned not to depend on others. It's an old habit, I'm afraid."

"Because of your past?"

"Probably," she conceded briskly. "Look, I really hate dwelling on the past. It can get positively maudlin, so why don't I tell you about some of the events I'm lining up for the kids?"

Reed sighed, reminding himself that this was just the first call. He couldn't expect to learn everything he wanted to know about Jade Howell in one fell swoop.

When he didn't say anything, she asked, "Would you rather talk another time? I don't want to keep you if you're busy."

The only thing he was busy with, he thought dryly, was another restless night. "Why don't you close up for the night and get on home?" Reed suggested, aware of the late hour. "I'll call again soon and we'll talk more about the center."

"All right."

Reed heard her doubt and responded to it. "Don't worry, Jade. I don't make promises if I don't plan to keep them, and I admire your commitment to the center."

It wasn't until after she hung up the phone and straightened her desk that she felt self-conscious about her openness with a total stranger. Even protected by the anonymity of the telephone, she felt an odd combination of relief and anxiety.

Perhaps he would call again. Perhaps he wouldn't. Perhaps he was just a crank with a few empty hours to kill, but she doubted it, although she wasn't totally certain why. She reminded herself to keep her expectations under control, but hope persisted and burned brightly within her.

Jade drove home via the post office. She listened to the night sounds of San Diego along the way. As in any large metropolitan community, police and ambulance sirens punctuated the darkness and relative quiet of modestly trafficked streets.

As she walked into her studio apartment, Jade realized that one of the reasons she worked such long hours was to avoid the loneliness of a home that resembled a motel room. On that less-than-comforting thought, she shed her clothes and crawled into bed. She didn't fall asleep easily or quickly, despite her fatigue.

"Lady, you give a man all kinds of wicked thoughts."

Jade smiled in spite of herself. The man who invaded her every thought, who arrogantly shoved aside the contents of her mind like so much refuse and then proceeded to take up permanent residence there, now stood in the doorway of her office. He leaned his shoulder against the frame and rested one hand on his hip, effectively bringing to mind a male centerfold. All he needed was to be stripped of his snug black T-shirt and even snugger jeans and the image would be perfect.

It wasn't possible, she thought. It simply wasn't possible to want a man as much as she wanted this man.

Reed moved forward into the sparsely furnished office with that confident loose-limbed walk of his. Nearly breathless, Jade charted the flex and give of the muscles of his strong thighs and wide chest. He didn't appear to have a single ounce of fat on his body, and she quickly decided that he must have a stomach as hard and as flat as a slab of stone. Her fingertips burned with the sudden desire to feel the warmth and vitality of his flesh. She paled at the thought.

"Mr. Townsend." She heard the tremor in her voice and fell silent.

"Ms. Howell," he answered, mocking her formal tone. "You look hungry... for me."

"You're outrageous," she spluttered.

He grinned. "That doesn't change the look on your face."

"Mr. Townsend!"

His grin widened at the warning note in her voice. "Yes, Ms. Howell?"

"Stop it. Please."

But she couldn't stop looking at him, although she did try. Her heart shifted when recognition—an astounding jumble of awareness, attraction and desire—arced along her nerve endings. In frustration, she noticed that her hands were shaking. She shoved them into her lap, but she could tell by the look on Reed's face that he'd already seen the betraying evidence of her emotional state.

He simply stood there, absorbing the feelings washing over him. His insides tightened, hunger flaring to life inside him as he felt a swift current of heat invade his bloodstream.

He noted with some pleasure that Jade looked stronger today. He thought about what had happened the day before. The color slowly stealing into her cheeks told him that she remembered, too. He also recalled their telephone conversation and felt a twinge of regret that he couldn't tell her the truth.

She saw the gleam in his eyes, a gleam that hinted at pure male satisfaction. Simmering in total silence, she watched him smile—that slow, deep smile of his that tightened her nerves and made her skin tingle. It was as though he'd reached out and touched her, stroked her, tantalized her with his eyes.

Jade wrenched herself free of his hypnotic gaze and glanced at her watch. "You must be done for the day."

"Not quite. You're hedging, you know."

She ignored his observation and asked, "How are you today?"

He looked at her, surprised and curious. "Great. You?"

"Wonderful, thank you."

Reed sank into the metal chair positioned in front of her desk, slouching low with one leg propped across his knee at the ankle. He dwarfed the chair, but it was the only way to conceal his body's response to her. On fire, he cursed himself for being so transparent.

"How about dinner tonight?"

She nodded, responding to a searing impulse that came out of nowhere to swamp her common sense. "I'd like that."

Startled, he sat taller in his chair.

Realizing that she'd finally gotten his attention, she wondered what she'd gotten herself into. "We need to talk about the center."

He nodded, his smile back in place. "Fine. What suits you in the food department?"

"Delfina's in Old Town?"

"Sounds good."

This is too easy, Reed thought. "Why?"

"Why what?" she asked.

"Why are you going out with me?"

"I just told you. We need to talk."

"Okay." He would figure it out later. "How was your day?"

"Very productive."

He glanced at the stack of envelopes piled high on her desk. "Donation requests for the center?"

"What else?"

"You don't give up, do you?"

"Never," she assured him.

The steel he'd heard before in her voice was back. He admired her commitment, but he also resented it. Her world was a one-focus operation. She didn't leave room for anything or anyone else.

"Any prospects on the horizon?"

"Yes, thank heavens." Her mind flitted to her anonymous caller. Hopefully she would hear from him again. Jade glanced at Reed and then at her hands. "I've decided we should forget what happened between us yesterday. It can't happen again. You do understand that, don't you, Mr. Townsend?"

He got to his feet, moved forward and then leaned down. With his hands placed firmly on the desk, he studied Jade for several silent seconds. "What happened yesterday couldn't have been avoided and can't be conveniently swept under the rug because it makes you feel uncomfortable."

"But it *will* be avoided in the future," she insisted. "And I'm not uncomfortable."

"We'll see." His look become noticeably speculative. "I think you are."

She exhaled softly as she eased back in her chair and folded her hands in her lap. "We're like vinegar and oil, Mr. Townsend."

"Reed."

"We're like vinegar and oil, Reed," she persisted. "It wouldn't work. We're too different."

"Don't you like vinaigrette?"

She laughed, the sound pure heaven to his ears.

"I love vinaigrette, but we're people, not salads."

He straightened abruptly, his frustration with her stubbornness mounting. "That's irrelevant."

"It's quite relevant."

"You don't like me."

Amazed by his comment, she searched his face and was relieved to see humor dancing in his beautiful eyes. "You're very nice . . . most of the time."

He winced. "'Nice'? What a word!"

"You're also . . ." She paused, not sure how to proceed.

"Go on."

"You're just more than I can handle right now. I'm not looking for a relationship with a man. In fact, it's the farthest thing from my mind at this point in my life."

"Is it?"

She knew he was mocking her. "Yes, it is," she insisted. Jade left her chair and wandered to the window that provided a fabulous view of the alley behind the center and several overturned trash cans. She felt the intensity of his gaze, but she didn't turn around. "I'm not equipped to deal with someone like you, Reed." You're too overpowering, she finished silently.

He swore softly, his expression suddenly grim as he charted her slim body with his eyes. Despite her attire—a pair of cotton leggings and an oversize T-shirt—the hourglass shape of her figure was still evident. He remembered the narrowness of her back, the nothingness of her waist, hips that begged for a man's bracketing hands, and her breasts, surprisingly generous for her compactness. He would desire her until doomsday, of that he was absolutely certain.

Jade turned to face him. "I'm serious."

He nodded. "I know you are, and I even understand why." Reed knew they were worlds apart. She was like a newly minted coin, and he was tarnished in more ways than he cared to accept. Nothing could change that.

"Then you'll respect my feelings?"

Frustration resurfaced inside him, prompting him to bait her. "And what feelings are those?"

Jade experienced a spark of anger. "Our relationship can't progress beyond business and a casual friendship."

He smiled, almost bitterly. "Unless, of course, I'm pulling you out of the way of forklifts."

Jade felt her control snap. "No more grabbing, Mr. Townsend. No more jumping all over me, physically or verbally. Are we absolutely clear on that?"

"You're coming through loud and clear, Jade."

He stood, the grace and fluidity she was accustomed to seeing in his body when all those muscles and tendons and bones moved in incredible harmony now absent.

She spoke softly, sensing that she'd said something hurtful but unaware of exactly what. "I don't mean to offend you, but I don't want you to have the wrong idea about me. The center takes all my time and energy."

She was lonely and afraid. That thought came right out of the blue. Given what she'd revealed the night before, it should have occurred to him sooner. Anonymity was fast becoming a double-edged sword.

"I've never forced a woman in my life, Jade. I don't plan to start now."

He towered over her. She had the random thought that she should start wearing high heels, but even that wouldn't help. His sheer bigness simultaneously served as an invitation and a warning. Wanting him was so effortless, but she knew better than to indulge herself. Jade unconsciously pressed her hands to her sides.

"Reed, I'm not accusing you of force."

"Then what are you implying? You'll have to spell it out for me."

Confused, she replied, "I meant what I said. There's no space in my life for a relationship."

He shrugged, feigning an indifference he didn't feel. "You're lying, but if that's how you want to play this out, fine."

"I'm not playing or lying."

"Aren't you?" He took a step closer, encompassing her in his personal space. A muscle bunched in his jaw.

Anger flared again inside her. "I've already told you that macho doesn't do a thing for me."

He leaned down until they were simply passing an invisible wedge of air back and forth between them. "Don't lie, Jade. You get very pale every time you do it, and it's a dead giveaway."

She stepped back and bumped into the wall.

Reed saw shock and fear in her eyes and moved away. He struggled to remind himself of a conclusion that he'd come to just seconds ago. She wasn't afraid of him; she was afraid of herself.

He held his hands out in front of him in a conciliatory gesture. "I won't push you."

The woman who had survived orphanages and foster homes emerged. "I'll push right back if you do, so be warned."

He exhaled sharply, attracted to her sudden burst of temper. Nerve endings in his body leaped to life again. "I think I'd like it if you pushed back, but I won't push you unless you ask me to."

She didn't address the suggestive double meaning contained in his comment. "You're sure?"

"It'll kill me, but yes."

She looked genuinely confused. "Kill you?" she repeated.

His voice, already rough and low, went a full tone deeper. He sounded wild and untamed as he spoke. "I want you, lady. I want you naked and in my bed. I want you under me, on top of me and beside me. Most of all, I want to lose myself inside you. Am I making myself clear, Jade? I want you any way I can have you, but that doesn't mean I won't respect your wishes. I'm not a complete bastard."

Staggered by his bluntness, she demanded, "Has anyone ever told you how utterly tactless you are most of the time?"

"I'm an honest man, Jade, and I don't run from my emotions." He walked to the door. "I'll pick you up at seven."

She shook her head and then amazed herself when she said, "No. I'll meet you there."

He paused in the doorway before slowly turning to face her. She was always hiding. "If that's what you want."

She nodded, that stubborn look Reed knew so well in her expression again.

"My mother and my sisters—"

"What!"

He grinned, blatantly delighted that he could throw her off balance so easily. "They think I'm tactless, too, but they still love me."

Jade leaned back against the windowsill, a distinct softening taking place in her heart. "I'm glad your mother and your sisters love you, Reed."

Jade watched him change before her eyes. His countenance grew harsh and cold, his body rigid. She drew in a breath so quickly that her lungs hurt for a moment.

"My ex-wife said she loved me, too, but that didn't keep her from sleeping around."

On that harsh note, he departed. Stunned, Jade nearly sagged to the floor.

Three

Glancing in the mirror fastened to the back of the closet door, Jade nervously checked her appearance one last time. She knew the simple outfit she wore—a short, gathered skirt, a boxy top in a matching navy-and-white silk print and low-heeled white sandals—would be appropriate for dinner at Delfina's on a warm summer evening.

After fastening large gold hoops to her ears and dabbing cologne on her pulse points, she grabbed her white straw shoulder bag, a memento of a Sunday afternoon spent bargain hunting in Tijuana, and headed for the door. She walked the short distance from her apartment to the restaurant in less than ten minutes, reminding herself with each step she took that this wasn't really an official date.

If anything, she reasoned, having dinner with Reed in a public place would muffle his outrageous tongue, help her clarify her deadline for final payment on the construction work being done at the center and reinforce her determination that their relationship would remain platonic.

The sound of a strolling mariachi band warned her that she'd entered Old Town, an area in San Diego popular with both the locals and tourists.

Reed stood at the entrance to the open-air restaurant and bar, a bottle of beer in his hand and a smile on his tanned face as he chatted with other patrons. Jade's steps slowed when she spotted him. Clad in white slacks, a soft rose-colored polo shirt and leather huaraches, he appeared at ease in the milling crowd.

He took her breath away when his smile broadened into a wide grin as she approached him. When he drew her into his arms for a quick hug, Jade nearly forgot her vow to remain aloof and casual.

Easing her back a few feet, he proceeded to look her over from head to toe before declaring, "You look good enough to eat, Ms. Howell."

She flushed a brilliant shade of red when several people nearby chuckled at his remark. Jade briefly considered digging a hole in the cement below her feet as the color receded from her cheeks.

"You're impossible," she chided with a rueful smile.

He gave her a look that reminded her of a hungry predator stalking his prey. "There are some things in this life that you can always count on." After taking a healthy swig of his beer, he handed the empty bottle to a passing waiter.

Smiling down at her, Reed reeled her back in against his hard body and slipped his arm around her waist. It didn't even occur to Jade to resist his possessive behavior.

Leading her into the bar, he settled her into a chair at a reserved table. A cocktail waitress immediately appeared. Jade wasn't surprised by the prompt service. How many women could ignore Reed Townsend? She certainly hadn't been able to.

"What would you like to drink?"

"White wine, please."

Reed nodded and gave their order to the woman.

"You just washed your hair. It smells like fresh honeysuckle."

"Thank you, I think." She wondered what he would come up with next.

Reed reached out and took her hands. After untangling her fingers, he ran his index fingers back and forth across her palm. Jade felt his touch deep in the marrow of her bones.

"Nervous?"

She frowned and jerked her hand free. "Of course not."

"You needn't be, you know." He winked at her and eased back in his chair. "Too many people around for me to pounce on you."

She laughed helplessly, the nervousness she'd just denied disappearing like a wisp of smoke.

After that, Reed settled down. Jade knew she shouldn't have been surprised by his easygoing charm but she was, anyway. He slowly disarmed her, chatting about inconsequential topics as they lingered over their drinks.

When their waitress led them to another reserved table, this time in the dining area, neither of them bothered with menus. They nibbled fresh tortilla chips smothered in cheese, guacamole and a spicy salsa while they waited for the mouth-watering enchiladas, refried beans and steamed rice Delfina's was known for.

As they ate, they talked books and politics. Jade learned of Reed's passion for the same authors she enjoyed, and discovered, to their mutual surprise, that they held similar political views as well.

They also discussed architectural design. Jade expressed her preference for vaulted ceilings, long walls of tall windows, and hardwood floors. Reed concluded that she'd had little personal territory to call her own during her growing-up years. He also realized that she'd just described his sprawling beachfront home in Del Mar.

She shocked him only once during dinner when she admitted that she'd sold her condominium the previous year in order to come up with sufficient funds to start the Activity Center. It seemed that the volatile San Diego real-estate market periodically produced, instead of depleted, modest nest eggs.

She explained that she didn't want to use any of the center's donated monies for her own salary for the first few years, so she'd invested a portion of her equity in order to produce a small income for living expenses. Astounded by the extent of her personal and professional commitment to the children served by the center, Reed silently repledged himself to annual contributions to the Activity Center.

Much to her chagrin, Jade realized halfway through their meal that there wasn't anything about Reed that she didn't like. His rough charm delighted her, but she found she appreciated him most when he described his family. His mother sounded like a traditional mom who loved her children to distraction.

His sisters—one older and one younger—were both married and had children. He spoke of them in a voice filled with amused tolerance—typical, Jade imagined, of most brothers. According to Reed, their husbands—one a lawyer and one a doctor—were stable and responsible men. When he didn't say anything about his father, she assumed the omission was simply an oversight.

"You haven't mentioned your father," she noted after taking a sip of wine.

Reed put his fork down and leaned back in his chair. The sudden lack of animation in his expression startled Jade.

"I'm sorry. I didn't mean to pry."

He shook his head. "No problem. He's dead. Has been for several years."

She recalled the death of her own parents and felt a surge of empathy for Reed. "It must have been difficult for you."

"It was a relief," he told her in a tone lacking even the barest hint of emotion. "The only difficult part was that he nearly destroyed everything in his path before he finally checked out. He was a bastard, through and through."

Compassion prompted her to say, "I can't imagine what that must have been like for you and your family."

Despite his tension, Reed shrugged and reclaimed his fork. "The end of one person's life sometimes means the beginning of life for others."

His cryptic remark left her with an even greater sense of uncertainty. Although she toyed with the idea of asking him about his marriage, she quickly decided against it. She'd already cast a pall on their dinner with her last question.

Besides, she didn't really want to think of him with other women, not even a wife. That realization brought her up short. But so did the constant heat in Reed's gaze and the silent sizzle of awareness that surrounded them and reminded her of an invisible magnetic field.

Reed regained his poise as he listened to Jade chat about a particularly quirky reporter who had interviewed her for a local news station in the early days of the center. Her attempt to divert him from his dark thoughts was obvious, but he didn't mind. Any talk of his late father always left him feeling the pain that had nearly destroyed him as a young man and had driven him from home at an early age.

Having devoted time and energy to coming to terms with his violent childhood, he didn't expect to ever forgive the man who had also used his fists on his wife and daughters. Nor could he absolve his father of guilt for nearly destroying Foothills Construction, a company founded by Reed's maternal grandfather.

The success of the construction firm now exceeded anyone's wildest fantasies, and Reed took pride in what he'd accomplished since taking over the company. Following his father's suicide, he'd resigned from the Marine Corps, returned home and guided the floundering family-owned company from the edge of bankruptcy to its current place as a major corporate presence in Southern California.

That Jade would question him about his father left him with mixed feelings—appreciation and surprise that she cared enough to ask, but concern that she would think less of him because he didn't possess the charity to mourn his natural father or the ability to forgive the man.

Replete after a filling meal, they agreed to pass on an after-dinner drink in Delfina's crowded bar. Reed escorted Jade to the restaurant exit, his arm around her waist as they stepped out onto the sidewalk.

She glanced up at him as they walked down the street. "We didn't discuss one aspect of the center that still concerns me."

His arm tightened. Jade felt the flex and flow of muscle in his body as he brought her to a halt and turned her so that they faced each other. Despite the dim light of a nearby streetlamp, she could see the sober expression on his face.

"Is it something I said?" she asked lightly, surprised by the sudden tension in him.

"Tonight isn't about business." He gave her a look guaranteed to scorch her soul. "I want you."

Startled by his bluntness now that her defenses were in total disarray, she tried to pull free. His fingers instantly tightened. She stopped struggling when she saw the smoldering desire in his dark eyes. Wary and uncertain, she waited for him to speak. She also waited for her heartbeat to return to normal.

"Don't pull away from me, Jade." He threw his head back, the corded muscles of his neck revealing his inner struggle. "My God! You can't even begin to imagine the things I want to do to you, can you?" Images filled his mind—images that made his body tighten and his blood run so hot that he fought a major internal battle for control.

"Reed, please—"

"Please what? Please disappear from my life? Please take me to bed and put an end to this ache inside me that I keep fighting? Please what, Jade?" he demanded ruthlessly.

She flinched. "I thought I made myself clear this afternoon. I can't offer you anything other than my friendship."

He abruptly released her, dropping his hands to his sides. Shaken by his constant unpredictability, Jade stared at him.

"I'm just trying to be honest with you," she insisted stubbornly.

"Are you being honest with yourself?"

"Reed—"

"What do you want to talk about?" he cut in.

"The completion date on the center," Jade clarified. "If the September 15th date is subject to change, I'll need to know."

He stiffened. "The contract says the 15th. I bring my jobs in on schedule."

"I didn't mean to imply that you didn't."

"What else?"

She studied him, desperate to ease the tension that had invaded his body and to erase the cold look on his face. "I really would like to be your friend," she whispered.

Some of his frustration subsided but not all of it. It finally occurred to him that she needed to believe what she was saying.

"Lady, I don't think you know what you want."

"We're destined to go in circles on this topic forever, aren't we?" She sighed softly and glanced at her watch. "Look, it's late. I should get home."

"How do you feel about the piano bar at the Hilton?"

Confusion prompted her to admit, "I didn't know they had one."

"An hour, Jade. Give me another hour. I won't ask for anything more tonight."

She hesitated. She didn't really want to go home to her empty apartment, but could she risk the volatility seething between them?

Jade responded to impulse rather than common sense. "All right. Another hour."

He nodded, remaining silent because he didn't want her to change her mind, and then led her to his car. The drive to the Mission Bay hotel only took a few minutes on the freeway.

Reed pulled into the parking lot, turned off the ignition and reached for the door handle. Jade reached out too, but not for the purse resting on the floorboards beside her feet; she let her fingers come to rest on his wrist.

Reed stiffened, made himself breathe deeply, and wondered how even her slightest touch could be so incendiary. He turned to face her, feigning a calm he didn't feel as he settled back in the leather bucket seat of the sports car. "Something wrong?"

"No," she whispered. Her eyes, so wide and so achingly vulnerable, dominated her face.

The tempting thought of touching him barreled through her mind like an out-of-control freight train, obliterating once and for all any restraint she possessed at that moment in time.

Thought became reality. Reality became a sensory quest.

She lifted her hand and brought it to his hard cheek. The tips of her fingers came to rest at his temple. She felt a muscle in his jaw shift under her touch. Such warm skin, she mused as the pulse in his temple beat a wild tattoo against her fingertips.

"You're risking a lot right now."

She almost didn't recognize his voice because it was so ragged and low, but she did realize what he meant and started to lower her hand. He seized it and held it in place, pressing her palm to the unyielding sinew and bone beneath the masculine roughness of the skin stretched tautly across his cheekbone. He closed his eyes, savoring their physical contact, the first Jade had willingly initiated herself.

Emotion-charged currents arced wildly inside her, bringing with them the warning sting of tears. Frustration and desire lashed her heart. Heat pooled deep inside her. She trembled ever so slightly. Reed felt the delicate shudders and hope rekindled inside him.

"I didn't mean to offend you before, and I don't want to hurt you," she whispered. "I really don't."

He exhaled heavily and opened his eyes. Drawing air back into his starved lungs, he renewed his acquaintance with the delicate fragrance of her skin when he tugged her forward and pressed his lips to the side of her neck. The silk of her shoulder-length hair caressed his face, the heat of her soft flesh shook his self-control.

He reluctantly pulled away a few moments later, the need in him so raw, so desperately primitive, that he knew he was on the verge of exploding. "Let's take a walk down by the water."

Still shaken by his touch, Jade exited the car. She didn't protest when he took her hand and led her down one of the winding paths of the public park adjacent to the hotel's grounds. They walked in silence for several minutes, both only vaguely aware of the sailboats, their running lights tiny beacons in the darkness, slipping soundlessly through the serene waters of Mission Bay.

Reed finally suggested a brandy in the piano bar before calling it a night. Jade readily agreed. Although deeply troubled by her response to him, she still felt a certain reluctance to the idea of ending their evening together. She also felt torn between what she knew she should do and what she *wanted* to do.

It would be so easy, she realized, to abandon her common sense and hurl herself into a full-fledged affair with this man, but she knew she couldn't. The Activity Center had to remain the focus of her time and attention. And the risk inherent in needing or trusting another person with her emotions, even if the temptation to do so was staggering, still seemed impossible to her.

The music in the piano bar was too appealing to ignore. Jade slipped into Reed's arms on the dance floor with the ease of a longtime lover gliding into her mate's embrace. He moved with the competent grace of a man comfortable with his size. As he guided her skillfully, their bodies moved in splendid harmony to a series of haunting love songs.

Jade wasn't certain when things began to change. She lost track of time. She lost track of the other people in the piano bar and on the dance floor. Most of all, she lost track of herself and all the reasons why she shouldn't be in Reed's arms.

He didn't speak. He simply held her, but with each minute that passed he grew more and more aroused. Unable to hide his response to her, he didn't bother to try. When Jade

pressed herself more firmly against him, he lowered his face
to the curve between her shoulder and neck, inhaling deeply
of her scent.

The tantalizing press of her full breasts made him shud-
der. He pulled her tightly to him, torturing himself further
with the curves and hollows of her lower body as their loins
met and imitated the ultimate mating experience. The insane urge to absorb her into his flesh took hold of him.

They barely moved in their tiny corner at the edge of the
dance floor. Instead they became one, swaying together in
an intimate embrace that resembled the foreplay of lovers so
intent on each other that the rest of the world simply faded
away.

Jade felt as though she'd been sucked into a whirlpool of
seduction. She had never experienced such an odd blending
of hunger and peace in the arms of a man. Startled by the
strength of her emotions, she trembled in Reed's embrace.

He sensed the change in her when he felt her burrow into
him. The impact of her growing breathlessness and the desire tremoring through her nearly brought him to his knees.
While he knew he was too mature and too rational to make
love to Jade in public, he briefly considered the merit of the
idea.

He couldn't take this self-imposed torture any longer. He
stopped suddenly. Jade glanced up at him in confusion, her
breathing erratic, her eyes wide with emotions Reed couldn't
even begin to name.

"I need some air," he finally managed.

"Yes," she agreed.

She let him guide her from the dance floor. Barely aware
of her actions, she reclaimed her purse while he dropped
several bills on the tabletop beside their untouched drinks.

They stood at the patio railing a few minutes later, each
caught up in the startling reality of what had just occurred.

"We were close to making love in there."

Jade heard the shock and anger in his voice. She risked a glance and watched him press the heels of his palms to his eyes. She felt his agony because she suffered from the same crippling desire.

"That was my fault. I got carried away."

"By the man or the music?" he asked as he lowered his hands to the wrought-iron railing and gripped it until his fingers began to throb.

She sighed. "Both, I'm afraid."

"That's the bottom line, isn't it? Your fear."

She shook her head, her hair swinging back and forth under her chin. "I'm not afraid of you, Reed. I'm not afraid of anyone."

He laughed, the sound so bitter that she felt chill bumps rise on her skin despite the sultry heat of the summer night.

"I know that. Hell, you're afraid of yourself." He unpeeled his fingers from the railing and moved to stand behind her. "You're going to be the death of me, Jade."

"Not if we don't see each other again," she answered in a stark little voice that sliced his heart in half.

Reed drew her back against him and wrapped his arms around her. He held her still, waiting for the rigidity to leave her limbs. When she finally relaxed, he felt enormous relief. He also felt the weight of her breasts against his skin as he moved his crossed arms higher up her torso. He thought about the way her breasts had felt flush against him, her nipples like tiny twin daggers stabbing at his chest as they'd danced. Desire restaked its claim on him.

"It's a beautiful night, isn't it?"

He heard the strangled sound of her voice, but he couldn't discern the words. His heart, hammering out of control, and his pulse, now wildly accelerated, roared in his ears. Flattening his hands against her taut midriff, he began to stroke her beneath the loose top she wore.

Delicate muscles clenched in surprise under his fingers. He wondered about the more intimate muscles of her body and what they would feel like clenched around him. He groaned silently, the primitive sound echoing inside his skull.

The ascent of his fingers was slow and steady, tantalizing and soothing. Breathing erratically, Jade placed her hands over his just before he reached his goal.

Turning, she looked up at him. "We'd better stop this. We're going to drive each other crazy."

He gave her a pained smile and then dropped a quick kiss on her forehead. "Speak for yourself. I'm already crazed with need."

She stiffened, too caught up in the emotional and physical tumult he'd created to find humor in anything right now. "Don't tease me."

He realized what she meant as soon as the words left her mouth. She needed him to call a halt to this madness, but he was damned if he wanted to.

"I'm not a kid any longer, Jade. When I want a woman, I say so. And I want you. But when we make love, it'll happen because it's right for both of us, or it won't happen at all."

When? She drew her breath in sharply.

"Although I must admit I could take you right now with very little urging." He hugged her to him, his embrace as fierce as his voice. "I'd give my right arm to see you naked and bathed in moonlight." He lowered his head and whispered, "Open the doors, Jade, and let me inside."

"You don't know what you're asking."

Something in her voice made him loosen his hold on her and peer down at her pale face. The stark terror in her eyes

humbled him more than words ever could. A wealth of
protectiveness replaced the desire threatening his sanity.

Reed dropped Jade at her front door a short while later.
She thanked him for dinner in a sad and sober voice he
didn't understand, but he didn't push her. For all her inner
steel, she appeared as fragile as fine crystal as she stood in
her doorway and watched him drive away.

He paid the price for his restraint throughout the night.
By the time he crawled out of his bed at dawn, his nerves
were tied in knots and his body screamed for release.

Startled by the shouting voice coming from the interior of
the warehouse, Jade vaulted to her feet and raced out of her
office. With the lunch break still in progress, it had been
quiet during the preceding half hour. Now, though, it
sounded as if someone had gone berserk.

The shouting bounced off the high ceiling and smacked
her in the face as soon as she stepped into the warehouse.
Stumbling to a graceless halt, she located the source of the
noise.

Reed. She should have known.

Several of the men grouped around him noticed her.
They, too, seemed taken aback by his behavior. One of the
workers, a burly Latino man of indeterminate age, shrugged
as if to say, "Who knows what set him off?"

But Jade knew, because it was the same thing that had
kept her from a restful sleep. It had also made her edgy and
furious with herself. Marching toward him, her hands
formed into tight fists at her sides, she transferred her fury
to Reed.

"What in the name of heaven is going on in here?" she
demanded.

He saw her peripherally at first. A flash of bright red T-
shirt, that sleek shoulder-length mane of dark brown hair

swinging to and fro as she advanced on him, and those shapely legs of hers revealed by skimpy running shorts. Reed swung around to face her, his body language aggressive, the dark look on his face boding ill for anyone who ventured across his path.

"What the hell do you think you're doing? Get out of my construction area before I personally haul your fanny out of here," he roared. "I'm not gonna say it again, Ms. Howell. This won't be your turf until I say so. And stop wearing those blasted shorts. You're a walking invitation in that getup."

She glared at him, barely registering the departure, in groups of twos and threes, of the men who worked for Reed. He glared back at her, looking to all the world like some tawny jungle creature fresh from a frustrated hunt. She felt something snap inside her—something that separated her from clear thought and rational behavior.

"You conceited, overbearing, opinionated, chauvinistic jackass! How dare you speak to me in that tone of voice?"

Not interested in his reply, she turned on her heel and marched back down the long hallway to her office. She didn't even take the time to note the shocked looks on the faces of the men who had been their audience. Nor did she notice Reed's thunderstruck expression. She was too busy wondering why she'd let herself lose control. Thanks to Reed Townsend, she knew she'd sounded like some hissing, spitting alley cat. Damn the man!

She stood in front of her desk, the air streaming in and out of her lungs in uneven gasps. The door slammed behind her, startling her. She jerked around to confront him as bits of plaster fell like snow from the ceiling.

"Just because you didn't get . . . satisfied . . . last night is no reason to take your bad temper out on your men, Reed Townsend."

His expression hardened and his dark eyes, usually so
filled with sensual messages, turned wintry. Jade shivered
despite the stifling heat in the office.

"How the hell do you know what I did or didn't do last
night? I do know other women."

"I just bet you do!" Her withering tone could have dis-
abled an elephant.

Reed didn't miss a beat. "What's that supposed to
mean?"

"Your female friend, whoever she is, did a poor job of
relieving you of your obvious tensions, didn't she? Maybe
you should audition a new sex partner," she taunted. "The
one you've got obviously isn't working out."

"Lady," he muttered, stretching the word out until it
fairly hummed with tension.

Jade watched him advance toward her like some con-
quering monarch. "Stop right there, Reed. If you want to
play dictator, then you do it somewhere else. I'll be in my
grave before I'll ever allow you to pull this kind of thing
around here again. What if one of the children had wandered in here?"

"They don't belong here, either," he bellowed. Totally
disgusted with himself, he lurched for the door.

Alarmed by his behavior, Jade released a gust of air and
asked in a calmer tone, "What in the world's gotten into
you? You're acting like an out of control yo-yo."

He turned so slowly to face her that Jade felt she was
watching a slow-motion movie.

"You've gotten into me," he told her in a dangerously
low voice. "Now I want to get into you."

She flushed. "Don't be crude."

"You didn't think I was crude last night."

"A gentleman wouldn't—"

"I'm no gentleman. I'm just me, a construction jock who gets the job done—on time, with the best safety record in Southern California and without substandard building materials. I'm no gentleman, Jade," he repeated ruthlessly. "And I never will be."

"You're a gentleman when you want to be," she countered very quietly.

"You don't know what I am, and you don't want to find out. If you had the guts to discover the truth about me on your own, then I might understand if you decided to walk away. But you can't even do that, because you're a coward, Jade, a coward right down to the soles of your feet when it comes to trusting people."

"I'm a coward!" she exclaimed. "Well, that's no better than this Hitler act of yours. Your men idolize you, and you treat them like a bunch of irresponsible candidates for truancy."

He flinched, already keenly aware of how hard he'd come down on his crew for extending their lunch hour an extra few minutes. He owed every one of the men in the warehouse an apology, and they would all receive what they were due, but he wouldn't admit that fact to Jade.

"The treatment they receive from me is a direct result of their performance on the job. Nothing more, nothing less," he insisted stubbornly.

She threw her hands up in disgust. "Talking to you is absolutely hopeless."

"Then maybe we shouldn't talk." He prowled closer, his expression utterly primitive.

Jade refused to budge. "Fine. We won't talk."

He moved nearer. Jade saw a curious light shining in the depths of his navy blue eyes. Uneasiness sifted into her senses, alerting her to his change of tactics.

"There is no substitute for effective verbal communication, Reed."

He made a sound of pure disgust. "Is that something you learned in college, Ms. Howell?"

For the second time in three days, she felt like decking him, but she kept her fists pressed to her sides and refused to allow him to bait her further. She wouldn't sink to his level and fight like some street tough. Not even on a bet. Drawing herself up to her full five-feet, four-inch height, she tapped into the restraint that had helped her survive the past twenty-eight years.

"Mr. Townsend, come back when you've calmed down and can behave like a civilized person. Until then, I want nothing to do with you."

He grabbed her and jerked her forward until they were nose to nose. They glared at each other. And they both teetered on the edge of a steep emotional cliff, one that encouraged them to succumb to the temptation of responding to the intense wave of heat generated by their close proximity to one another.

"You're running away, Jade. You're running from yourself, and you're running from me. Oh, I know how different we are, so there's no need to keep reminding me. And I know I'm no knight in shining armor, but at least I'm not afraid to be myself."

Shaken, she all but whispered, "Let go of me, Reed."

He released her and stepped back, furious with himself and acutely aware of the fine line he now walked. He couldn't let Jade suspect that he might be her anonymous caller, but neither did he want his antagonistic bluntness to destroy the possibility of bridging the vast gulf between them.

Torn, he fired his final salvo. "Grow up, lady. Part of living is experiencing life, not hiding from it. Until you do that, you'll be worthless to yourself and to the kids you keep using as an excuse to go through life like some one-woman army."

Four

———

Reed sat on the floor in his living room. Slouched against the front edge of the couch with his long legs extended before him, he rested his head against the plump thickness of an overstuffed cushion. The darkness shrouding the California coastline reflected his somber mood.

He periodically took a sip of the bourbon he'd splashed into the bottom of a glass while he half listened to several taped messages on his phone recorder. The final message drew and held his attention.

"No need to worry about the Activity Center, old buddy. There'll be a unit out that way on a regular basis unless an emergency is declared and our manpower has to be redeployed. Give me a call next week and we'll play some poker." David Henderson chuckled softly. "Must be some kinda special lady down there to get your attention like this."

The dial tone sounded, and Reed lifted his drink in salute to his old friend. David, now a detective in homicide with the San Diego Police Department, knew him well. They had caroused together as troubled teens, run off and joined the Marine Corps and then trained and served for five years in an elite antiterrorist unit. A time-tested friendship and the blood of their fallen comrades bound them together in ways few people would ever comprehend.

Reed shook his head in frustration, rewound the message tape and then pushed his drink onto the coffee table beside him. David was right. Jade *was* special—too special to be at risk in a high-crime area at night.

He didn't begrudge his friend his insightful observation, although he did frequently begrudge Jade her carelessness when it came to her own personal security. Short of calling in a favor from a friend in law enforcement, as he'd done with David, or standing guard over her himself, which she would fight tooth and nail just on general principle, he knew there was nothing he could really do to convince her to be more careful.

Reed reached for the phone, his thoughts on the lady in question. He'd pushed her today. Hard. He knew that, but he also knew the necessity for his actions. He couldn't risk her discovering the secret side of his life.

Since Foothills Construction had regained its financial health, he'd selectively become an anonymous benefactor to several local charities. Anonymity was the only condition he ever set on his generosity, and all the charities served the needs of children.

Reed tapped out the digits that would connect him to Jade's office at the Activity Center. He settled back against the couch as the phone rang, still surrounded by the darkness and still feeling isolated by the dual roles he'd chosen to play.

Worry built inside him like a dammed-up stream by the ninth ring. When Jade finally picked up the receiver on the eleventh ring, Reed felt his gut clench with relief at the sound of her breathless voice.

"Activity Center."

He didn't speak for a moment. She sounded soft and vulnerable, as vulnerable as she had looked when he'd stormed out of the center earlier in the day. He didn't think he would ever forget the hurt shimmering in her doelike eyes, nor would he forget the pain twisting in his own chest when he'd accused her of emotional cowardice.

The blows he'd delivered had been low. He knew that, but he sensed that shock tactics were necessary with Jade. Perhaps tonight he would better understand her reticence, her denial of their mutual attraction to each other. He desperately needed to understand. He also felt compelled to trust his instincts where she was concerned. Those same instincts had been the key to his emotional and physical survival for many years. He prayed they would continue to serve him well.

"Activity Center," Jade repeated. "May I help you?"

Reed slid the folded bandanna into place over the phone to distort the sound of his voice. He exhaled quietly before he spoke. "Miss Howell?"

"Yes?"

"How are you this evening?"

Jade sank into her chair, warmth washing gently through her as she recognized his subdued voice. "I'm just fine. And you?"

He heard the softening, the welcome in her tone. "Good, thanks. I just came in from the beach."

"A walk at the edge of the ocean as the sun sets," she guessed aloud.

"Not quite," Reed admitted, smiling at the romantic image her comment provoked. "I try to run a few miles every night. It keeps me in shape."

"If you're cooped up in an office all day, then I imagine you look forward to getting outside for some exercise."

He realized she was fishing. "That's a reasonable deduction." He shifted uncomfortably, hating that he had to be so evasive with her. "Shall we talk more about the center?"

She was pleased that he hadn't taken offense at her curiosity. "I'd like that, but before we begin, would you answer a question for me?"

"If I can."

Once again Jade noted his caution. Perhaps someone had hurt him once, and he'd never really gotten over it. Or maybe he really did like his privacy. "You do live at the beach, don't you?"

"Yes. Should I assume that you have a particular fondness for it, too?"

She laughed. "As a matter of fact, I do."

"Then we have something else in common, don't we?"

She suddenly felt shy, despite the fact that he was simply referring to the center and the beach. She wished they could speak face-to-face, as friends would. That thought startled her, but she accepted the notion her subconscious had just produced with little resistance. Since his first call, hadn't she wanted to think of him as a potential friend?

"I get the feeling we have a great deal in common."

"You're right, Jade. We do."

His admission sounded somewhat sad, even forlorn, and she wondered why. Some second sense told her that she could trust him, though. If asked why, she doubted that she would be able to come up with reasoning based on anything more tangible than instinct and feminine intuition, but that would do for the time being.

She turned her attention to the purpose of his call. "I've been working on grant applications since we last spoke, and I've also had a chance to compile a list of the activities tentatively scheduled for the center immediately following our grand opening."

"Tell me," he invited, his tone still pensive.

"Well, to start with, I've lined up several local athletic equipment distributors who have agreed to donate supplies for the children. In conjunction with that, I've spent the past month recruiting coaches and PE teachers from several schools in the area to volunteer one afternoon each month to teach the kids how to use the equipment properly. Twenty have already signed up. We'll have a monthly schedule filled out in no time. They'll work in two-person teams for three hours each afternoon during the week and all day on Saturday."

She glanced at her list, proud of what she'd accomplished. "The Padres management people have guaranteed us a block of tickets for games through the end of the baseball season, the Chargers have offered us a dozen seats for a November home game, and the zoo, the Wild Animal Park and Sea World have all promised field trips for the children.

Reed discovered a deep well of pride within himself with Jade's name on it. "You've been busy, haven't you?"

"Our plans are all finally starting to come together."

"Am I correct in assuming you have age restrictions at the center?"

"Yes. From a legal standpoint, it's a must. We're focusing on school-age children from six to eighteen. It takes special licensing to run a child-care facility for the younger ones, and their needs are quite specialized. Sometimes a little one will wander in with an older brother or sister, and we don't take issue when it happens. Neither do we encourage it, but the kids have learned out of sheer necessity to look out for their younger siblings."

"Who looked out for you?" Reed asked without considering how intrusive the question might sound.

"I did," she answered, her tone suddenly cool and detached.

He frowned. "No friends at all?"

"Not really."

"Too transient an environment?" he pressed gently.

"That's right. Plus too painful when you got yanked out of the orphanage to become a maid for a foster family, or if the foster family got bored with the novelty of having you around. I had childhood asthma. I'm over it now, of course, but it certainly didn't endear me to anyone when I had an attack."

He felt the tension in her thanks to the staccato quality of her reply. And his respect for her multiplied tenfold, because he knew how reluctant she was to discuss her personal life or her past. "I'm impressed by both the reasons for and the strength of your convictions concerning the center, Jade, but I think we need to move on to your fundraising efforts now."

She slumped into her chair, relieved to shift attention away from herself. Eager to get to the topic of funding, she was glad he'd brought it up. It was still the toughest part of her job. She didn't enjoy begging for money, but she never let her pride get in the way and forced herself to do it.

"Since starting the center a year ago, I've filled out enough federal and foundation grant applications to sink a battleship. The process is tedious, at best, but I'm hopeful that we'll get a positive response and additional funding in the near future. We've had three fund-raisers sponsored by local charitable organizations, and a San Diego bank is handling a modest trickle of private donations. Our media exposure has been hit-and-miss, but I'm working on changing that.''

"Why not hire a professional fund-raiser?"

She shook her head, so strong were her feelings on the subject, right or wrong. "The money pledged by the public generally gets spent on overhead. I don't want to waste one penny of donation dollars on salaries, no matter how clever the people involved might be."

"I understand your skepticism, but I think you may be overextending yourself."

"My being overextended isn't the issue."

Reed didn't miss the edge in her voice, but he ignored it. "Yes, Jade, it is. If you burn yourself out fund-raising for the center, of what use will you be to the children?"

"I won't burn out," she insisted stubbornly. "I'm committed, body and soul, to making the center work for the children it's designed to serve. Look, if we can attract the interest of consistent contributors who are willing to become personally involved with their dollars and their time, then we'll have a committed community behind us. I believe in the people of San Diego, and I want the center to reflect their generosity. And once the dollars are lined up, I'll be able to spend more time with the kids."

"You really think that's possible?"

His skepticism upset her more than she wanted to admit. "Absolutely. *You're* interested in helping us, aren't you?" she asked as a means of reinforcing her reasoning. "And if you care, then others will, too."

"Perhaps."

"You do care! I know you do."

Jade's obvious alarm and worry made his voice sharp as he asked, "What's wrong?"

She exhaled heavily, too upset to realize that Reed had just unwittingly let his guard slip. "Nothing other than long hours and a rough day."

He ached inside, aware that he was the primary cause of her rough day. "You're proving my point."

"Not intentionally."

He laughed at the wryness in her voice, almost dropping the swatch of fabric he held over the receiver. He hastily repositioned it. "Perhaps you should consider changing your tactics."

Jade shook her head—the expression on her face, the stubborn set of her chin, clear indicators of her determination. "I don't think so."

"We're back to being in total control, aren't we?"

"Think of it as guiding a ship. Having more than one captain gets complicated."

"Twenty-four hours a day?" he asked.

"If need be."

"That doesn't allow you time for a private life."

She thought of Reed in that instant. His face appeared in her mind with amazing clarity, but she pushed his image away. She wanted him, certainly, but she couldn't have him. He would expect much more than she was able to give in a relationship.

Already frustrated because Reed was slowly but surely mowing down her resistance to him and resentful because he already possessed a healthy chunk of her emotions, she didn't know what to do about him. Drawn to him despite her attempts to smother her unruly feelings, Jade had the uneasy premonition that she was on the verge of abandoning all her good sense where he was concerned. Fighting this inclination now consumed much of her energy and thought. She cared deeply about him, but she sensed that he could jeopardize the emotional stability she'd spent several years building.

"My life is the center," she insisted, her tone forceful but also tinged with regret.

"That's unfortunate."

She frowned, not expecting such an observation. "Why?"

Reed purposely misquoted a timeworn phrase. "No woman is an island."

"I'm not an island. I'm surrounded by children. At least I will be again, once the reconstruction work is finished."

"I find it difficult to believe that there isn't someone in your life."

She cleared her throat, the sound an unintentional betrayal of her nervousness. His insightful comment threw her off balance, almost in the same way that Reed's persistence did. She decided that the two men had blunt honesty in common.

"I apologize. I shouldn't have said that."

"No, it's all right. My life's a tad complicated at the moment."

He exhaled with a slightly muffled sound. "Tell me a bit about yourself, Jade."

She groaned silently. "I pretty well covered everything when we talked the other night."

No, he reflected. You gave me an encapsulated version of the life of a frightened little girl who spent her childhood being passed around like a roll of paper towels at a picnic. Only her childhood hadn't been a picnic. More like a lonely nightmare, he suspected, especially after the way she'd glossed over those empty years when they'd first talked.

"Did you put yourself through college?" he asked when she didn't fill in the silence.

"Why, yes, I did," she answered. "A partial scholarship and working full-time paid the bills. I managed to qualify for a study grant for my graduate work."

"You were and are quite ambitious."

"No, not really. I just saw what I had to do if I wanted my independence."

"Your degrees are in social work, aren't they?"

"Yes, but how did you know?"

Good, Townsend. Simply tell the woman you've been nosing around her office. That'll inspire confidence in a big way. After searching his thoughts, he came up with what he hoped would be a good bluff. "I seem to recall an article in the *San Diego Union* last spring about the center. The reporter included your academic credentials in the biographical segment of your interview."

"I'd forgotten about that. You have a quite a memory."

No, he thought. He had a driving need to know everything about the woman, Jade Howell. "Did you think you could change the system that neglected you as a child?"

God, he knew her too well! "I had high hopes, but I was incredibly naive."

"It's difficult to accept the reality of the world some of the time, isn't it?" Reed drained the bourbon from his glass and wished for more.

She sighed softly, but he heard the sound anyway.

"No need to answer that last question."

"I already did, didn't I?"

"I suppose you did," he agreed, striving for a mild tone while trying to control the urge sweeping through him that encouraged him to offer the safe haven of his arms.

"Would you answer another question for me?" Jade asked cautiously.

"What would you like to know? Aside from my identity, of course."

"Are you from San Diego?"

"I grew up here, and I was gone for several years after I finished high school. My family is fourth-generation San Diego, so I guess that makes me a native." He recalled his father and the reasons for his departure, which brought to mind a nagging concern he had regarding the center. "I have a question for you now."

"Ask away," she encouraged.

"When you described your plans for the center the other night, you mentioned counseling for the children. Were you referring to mental health specialists, or were you speaking in more general terms?"

"The former," she explained. "These kids are under a very special kind of pressure. So are their parents." Reading between the lines, Jade pursued what he'd begun. "Is the availability of specialized counseling important to you?"

"Extremely."

His one-word answer held a wealth of unstated emotion. Jade, already receptive to her caller for reasons she couldn't yet define, sensed the significance of the moment. Her concern that she might somehow offend him kept her from saying anything for several moments.

"What are you thinking, Jade?"

"That I'm glad you care about the children and the center," she answered, feeling clumsy. "Whatever your motivation."

Reed knew it was now or never. Other than David Henderson, no one knew his personal history. He dug deep inside himself for the courage he needed. Baring his soul was not something he did easily or well. But with Jade he felt the necessity of as much honesty as he could muster, given the unusual circumstances of their dual relationship.

"My motivation," he began with some difficulty, "is based on personal experience—not as a homeless person, but as a man who spent his childhood in a home filled with anger and violence. I didn't have anyone to go to when my father physically abused me. As a result, I want to be assured that the children served by the center have a resource if they're being victimized. I also want your personal assurance that all of the volunteers at the center will be trained to watch for the signs of child abuse." Air seesawed in and out of him, and an odd blending of relief and embarrassment fused inside him.

Unable to speak, Jade wept silently. Finally pulling herself together, she riffled her purse for a tissue and managed, "I'm not sure what to say, except that I'm sorry."

His heart nearly shattered when he heard her tear-soaked voice. "Don't cry for me, Jade, and don't be sorry. I'm over it. More important, I survived it."

She felt truly humbled by his trust with such a painful and private issue, and she also experienced a greater understanding of his desire for anonymity. She had no way, of course, of discovering his identity, but she suspected that he wasn't simply a survivor, but a proud man of innate strength and compassion.

"Would you be offended," she asked, "if I tell you that I think you're a better person for what you've experienced? Your past could have easily made you bitter and angry, but instead it's increased your sensitivity to the needs of others. That makes you quite unique in my book."

"I do care, Jade, but don't try and make me into some kind of a hero, because I'm not," he told her gruffly, still shaken by his frankness. He couldn't help but wonder how she would have responded if the Reed Townsend she knew had confessed the same truths about himself. "Being helpless and being victimized is a terrifying experience, especially for a child. It's also a cruel way to grow up, although I do realize that most people aren't born cruel. They simply get pushed to the edge by circumstances they can't control, or they're too weak to keep themselves from crossing the line that separates the rational from the irrational.''

"You didn't have *anyone* to turn to?"

He thought about his mother and his sisters, also victims, and then he thought about the Marine Corps family he'd become a part of, but he couldn't mention any of it. Jade knew that Reed Townsend had served in the corps. He searched his mind and discovered a noncommittal reply. "I found a way out."

"I'm so glad," she breathed.

"We have a lot in common, you know."

Shocked, she straightened in her chair. "I was never abused."

He knew she was fighting the truth. "Perhaps not in a physical sense," Reed said gently.

The past that she wanted to forget swirled through her consciousness like a tornado. Four years old and no one to turn to, no one to soothe her fears, no one to explain why hugs and other expressions of affection were reserved for children with families; and no one interested in her dreams, her hopes, or her aspirations as she grew up.

She trembled under the force of her memories. His honesty had already struck a chord in her, and she realized instantly that she couldn't dishonor his trust by being less than candid. "You're talking about isolation and loneliness."

He heard the pain in her voice. "Jade, my father failed me, and the system apparently failed you, but we're both survivors. We may have lost our innocence as children, but we didn't fail ourselves. I think that's something to be proud of, but there is a big difference between the two of us."

"I don't suppose you're talking about the fact that you're a man and I'm a woman," she replied with false brightness.

Reed ignored her attempt to divert him. He already knew all too well their physical differences—differences forever seared into his brain by the white-hot brand of thwarted desire.

"Your world is, by your own admission, limited to the center," he reminded her.

She wanted to hedge but found that with this man, who sounded profoundly world-weary and alone, she really couldn't. Her feelings about him had already slipped far beyond his potential as a source of funding for the center. And his honesty had signaled a shift in their relationship, on which she already placed a high value.

"I said it was complicated," she conceded.

"The only complication is your denial of your own needs."

"I can't get involved with anyone."

"Why not?" he demanded, deliberately soft-spoken.

"Because there's just not enough of me to go around!" she exclaimed. "Every ounce of energy and emotion I have has to go to the center."

"Why?" Even Reed heard the relentlessness of his quest for the truth.

How could she admit that she was desperately afraid of being abandoned by someone she let herself love? How could she tell her caller, a man of obvious courage, that *she* didn't possess the courage to take the chance? She dreaded the very thought of ever being vulnerable again.

"This doesn't really concern you." She told herself that she didn't care that she'd just taken the coward's way out, but deep in her heart she did.

Reed was silent for a moment. "You're right. It doesn't."

Regret instantly bloomed inside her. "I'm sorry. It's just that you've hit a nerve—one that someone else has been hammering on lately with incredible persistence."

He felt a very real pain in his chest at her indictment of his less-than-subtle tactics where she was concerned. "You don't have to explain."

She sighed in total frustration. "I couldn't, even if I wanted to. I don't understand what's happening, except that I've gone a little crazy over a guy who's so wrong for me it isn't even funny."

He briefly debated the wisdom of asking his next question and then plowed ahead into the fray he'd initiated. "How can caring about someone be wrong?"

"He would expect so much."

That startled him. "He's that demanding?"

"Not in the way you think." Jade shoved her fingers through her thick hair, ruffling her bangs as she tried to gather her thoughts. "He's like a tornado most of the time and he's definitely more than I can handle. He's brash, impossibly outspoken and completely unpredictable. He's also forceful and overwhelming, but I even like all those qualities because they fit him to a T. He makes me crazy, and he makes me laugh."

He also made her acutely aware of herself as a woman and incredibly hungry to know him as a lover, she realized for the hundredth time.

Reed heard a variety of emotions in her voice, but fear seemed to dominate. By risking further comment, he knew he risked alienating her. Nothing ventured, nothing gained, he decided. "You sound frightened."

"Oh, no! Not of him."

"Of yourself," he clarified, knowing full well the chance he was taking.

She fell silent, startled that in one day two people would come to that conclusion about her. When, she wondered, had her guard slipped? What had happened to make her so transparent?

"That's what he said," she told him in a voice so small that he almost missed her comment.

"Then I'm being redundant."

Trapped by her tangled emotions, Jade fought her panic. "Could . . . could we change the subject for now?"

Reed instantly pulled back. He'd pushed her again, more gently, of course, this time. But he sensed she couldn't deal with any more right now. "Certainly. In fact, it's late. Perhaps we should postpone the rest of our conversation until another time."

"I have plenty of time now," Jade hastily assured him. She seized the needs of the center as an avenue to reason and sanity. "In fact, I should be describing our budget. . . . Our nonexistent budget," she corrected with a rueful laugh. "And trying to convince you with numbers and facts just how desperate I am for donations to the center. My personal life is pretty dull stuff, if you want the truth."

He let her use the escape route she'd chosen. "That isn't necessary, you know."

"It isn't?"

"I'm aware of your need for operating capital to handle the center's monthly overhead expenses. Our conversations have simply given me a chance to get to know you more personally."

"Will you always insist on anonymity?"

"My desire to remain unidentified is no reflection on you or on my interest in the center, Jade."

"I'd still like to meet you. I already feel as though we're becoming friends."

"I really don't think that would be a good idea."

"Would you at least think about it?"

He paused, carefully weighing the situation.

"Please?" she whispered.

That single word, which sounded so much like a lover's entreaty, managed to blow a gaping hole in his common sense. "I'll think about it," he agreed reluctantly.

"Thank you."

Reed smiled bitterly, knowing that thanking him would be the farthest thing from her mind if she discovered the truth.

Feeling more lonely and isolated than ever, Jade spent yet another night steeped in conflict.

Reed constantly invaded the landscape of her consciousness. Her thoughts of him ran the gamut from bewilderment concerning the real reasons for his persistent campaign to seduce her to the unfulfilled promise in his darkly sensual eyes.

He waged a full-scale war in the confines of her mind, bulldozing her defenses in the same way that he'd bulldozed his way into her life. He shattered her emotional reserve. He tormented her. He aroused her. He drove her mad with wonder and worry.

He even slipped into her dreams when she drifted into the embrace of a fitful sleep, tormenting her further with erotic images that left her emotionally shaken and physically frustrated. Exhausted, she abandoned the idea of sleep well before dawn, but she remained in her solitary bed.

She needed to think, she reminded herself. She needed to ponder the ramifications of a relationship with Reed Townsend. She tried to be logical. She considered his unpredictable behavior, his hands-on, head-on-approach to every aspect of his life, including her; his forceful personality, his determined, pride-filled nature, his principles, and his high standards in the workplace.

He was, in a word, overwhelming. Even the continuous tug-of-war they waged didn't prevent him from personifying everything she admired in a man.

Logic danced in and out of her mind like a frantic fairy intent on driving her directly into Reed's powerful embrace. And despite all that she'd learned about him during the past few weeks, and despite the temptation to release herself from the emotional straitjacket she'd donned several years before, she still struggled to weigh the pros and cons of becoming involved with him.

Doubts and questions nagged at her as she considered giving in to the desire he inspired, the raging need to lose herself in his sensuality and strength, and the curious urging of her weary heart as it insisted that he was worthy of her trust. But her worry that she might be victimized by her own needs undercut her confidence and made her question his motives as dawn sprawled across the sky.

Was she simply a challenge to him? What if he grew bored? Wouldn't a dynamic man like Reed tire of her once he realized that she lacked the ability to be casual about an intimate relationship?

Would he think her tedious when he figured out that she needed much more than just sex from a man? Would he be shocked to discover how starved she was for someone to simply love her for herself? She sensed that behind his macho image was a man capable of infinite sensual tenderness; but was he capable of the patience she would need from him as she guided the Activity Center from dream to reality?

With all those questions swirling through her mind, Jade couldn't escape the fact that Reed, for all his verbal pushing and shoving, was right. Even her anonymous caller, a seemingly compassionate and kind man, was right.

She *was* afraid—afraid of needing, afraid of the vulnerability that would come with the commitment of her heart to another human being. She realized that allowing Reed into her life would be an admission of how deeply she cared for him and how important he'd become to her.

Jade knew the staggering risk involved. She knew not only because of the chain of events set in motion by the untimely deaths of her parents, but thanks to the risks she'd taken in the past.

Aside from a few occasions, which were etched into her soul, she'd kept secret her desperation for a family. Reticent and shy as a little girl, she'd mustered the courage to verbalize her yearning to be like other children.

She recalled that one time when she had innocently begged for parents. And she also recalled the swift, cutting hurt of disillusionment when the facts were explained to her in an emotionless tone of voice by the director of the orphanage.

Healthy babies, not sickly school-age kids, were wanted by adoptive parents. The truth of those words became reality when childless couples looked right through her and other grade-schoolers like her as they made a beeline to the orphanage nursery.

Still, she persisted. Convinced that she could win someone's love despite the evidence to the contrary at the orphanage, she hadn't given up. No one knew the heartache caused by the one foster mother she'd trusted when the woman had traded her in on a newer and better model once her asthma had developed into a full-scale medical problem.

Nor did anyone know about her first and only lover, the man who had swept her off her feet with promises of a wonderful life together shortly after she graduated from college. Ten months into their love affair, he claimed that wonderful life for himself by accepting a promotion and a transfer. He announced his impending departure with a quick phone call and a request that Jade help him pack for his cross-country move.

Deeply hurt both times, she covered her feelings of betrayal by refusing to let herself become emotionally involved again. She grew to view caring about others as a guaranteed journey to heartache, a trip to nowhere. Experience had already taught her that most people looked out for themselves, the rest of the world be damned.

Jade had tried to live that way after Mark's departure, but she couldn't quite bring herself to exist on such a self-centered emotional plateau. Becoming a part of the social services bureaucracy when she completed her graduate studies simply enhanced her frustration with her world. She slowly redefined her professional goals during the next four years.

Drawn to children who reminded her of herself, children who had, through no fault of their own, fallen through the proverbial social-services network cracks, children who lacked stability in their lives, she spent five years making the transition from social worker to founder and director of the fledgling Activity Center. The journey, she knew, had just begun, but she believed that the center would soon gain its financial footing.

While she held herself in check with most adults, she had little difficulty expressing her emotions with the children the center attracted. She saw their hunger for attention and responded to it. The woman in her responded, too. In small ways she did mother them just a little, because she gave them what she herself had longed for as a child: an adult they could count on.

Jade didn't blame their parents, who lived on the edge of society, with survival as the whole focus of their uncertain and transient existence. She didn't blame anyone, really. She simply wanted to make a small difference in their lives; and she wanted the children to know that they hadn't been forgotten.

Jade left her bed and made her way to the shower, her thoughts coming full circle. She experienced a stunning wave of inevitability as she stood beneath a pulsing stream of warm water and soaped her body. The fight had gone out of her sometime during the night, her resistance ebbing like a fleeing tide. Reed Townsend, without even realizing it, had punched a hole in her carefully constructed emotional armor.

She couldn't stop herself from wondering how she would feel, naked in Reed's arms, his hands mapping the curves and hollows of her body. She shivered at the thought of running her fingers along the corded muscles of his arms and powerful thighs, of testing the texture and give of the musculature that cloaked his broad chest and wide shoulders. She wondered, too, if she could infuse him with the same breathless, heart-stopping delight his touch had brought her.

Shocked by her wayward thoughts, she wished that she were a different person, maybe even a better and more complete person. Perhaps then she could reach out to a man like Reed Townsend. Whether or not she could actually grant him entrance into her insular world or access to her tightly tethered emotions, she didn't know. She'd considered the doors to her heart firmly sealed for so long.

Jade wasn't certain of anything as she dried herself, dressed, and applied a hint of color to her cheeks and lips. But deep inside, in the recesses of that fragile part of herself that she had learned to protect, was the burgeoning need to try again and the hunger to trust again, however harrowing the process had been in the past.

She pulled onto the freeway shortly before eight o'clock, joining the wall-to-wall rush-hour traffic inching toward downtown San Diego. She felt oddly detached, almost curious.

As she parked her car in the truck- and equipment-clogged parking lot behind the center, Jade fleetingly thought that it would be wonderful to find a combination of the personalities and characteristics of her anonymous caller and Reed Townsend. While each of them was unique, she suspected that a blend of two such distinctive men could certainly devastate every woman on the planet. It was such an odd, almost flighty notion that she laughed aloud, attracting the attention of two of the men who worked for Reed.

They waved and whistled when they saw her. Jade smiled and waved in return. The men, their wolf whistles and their waves of greeting, were a part of her morning routine. She didn't see Reed, who stood several yards away, watching her with an assessing look on his face.

Five

―――――

Jade carefully picked her way across the rutted parking lot behind the Activity Center and considered the folly of the decision she'd made while dressing for work. Instead of her usual shorts, T-shirt and athletic shoes, she wore a gray pencil-straight skirt, a crisp white blouse with cap sleeves and low-heeled pumps.

Reed's harsh criticism concerning her attire had bothered her. Despite the fact that she considered her clothing choices practical for the time renovation work was being done at the center, he'd managed to plant a seed of doubt in her mind. She rationalized her present outfit by reminding herself that as director of the Activity Center, a professional image was more desirable. Still, it rankled her that his opinions about her wardrobe even mattered.

She climbed a short flight of stairs, tugged open the heavy rear door of the warehouse and promptly stumbled into a bulky male figure. Taking a quick step backward, she gave him an inquiring look.

A short, middle-aged man, his bushy eyebrows corkscrewed in concentration as he scribbled on a notepad, stood like a misplaced fire hydrant in the middle of the doorway. A cloud of smoke drifted around his bald head as he puffed on the cigar clamped between his teeth. Sparing her a brief nod, he made a final note in the spiral pad before flipping it closed and tucking it into the breast pocket of his sport jacket.

Jade greeted him politely. "Hello. Are you lost?"

"Nope." He extended a chubby paw, engulfing her small hand as he briefly pumped it up and down. "Mick Everett. I expect you're Ms. Howell."

His name rang a familiar bell. "From the *Union*?" she asked eagerly.

"That's right. My editor wants a follow-up on the piece we did on the center last spring." He glanced around with sharp, experienced eyes. "Looks like you need the press."

Jade, delighted that the newspaper had responded so promptly to her phone call of earlier in the week, gave him a bright smile. "Would you like to see the renovations currently in progress, or would you prefer to interview me first, Mr. Everett?"

"Call me Mick, honey. Everybody does."

She immediately warmed to him, despite the grate of his gravelly voice. "All right, Mick."

"Let's do the warehouse first," he suggested briskly. "Then we'll talk."

He whirled around like a dervish at full tilt and headed back into the center. Jade raced along behind him, her stride hampered somewhat by her skirt. As she followed in his wake, she mentally blessed the newspaper editor who had dispatched Mick Everett, a talented features writer known for his human interest stories, to cover the center.

Finally, she thought, the tide was starting to turn in her favor.

Jade acted as a guide for the next hour, explaining as they went along her plans for various sections of the converted warehouse. She stressed the need for balance with the children who would come to the center, with equal attention, she pointed out, devoted to athletics and academic tutoring.

She credited the appropriate organizations already committed to the contribution of sports equipment and special field trips. She also outlined her plan to turn the parking area and weed-filled lot behind the center into a combination baseball diamond and football field once the renovation work was complete.

After telling him about the volunteers she'd managed to recruit, she completed her remarks with a gentle reminder that the center was wholly dependent on grants and the generosity of the local community for its financial survival.

Jade noticed Reed's absence during the extensive tour. Although she didn't have time to dwell on his reasons, she realized that even if he opted to act as foreman on her job, he still had the awesome responsibility of overseeing an extensive number of other construction projects scattered around Southern California.

Oddly enough, she still felt the need to share this small triumph with him.

After the tour, which was aided greatly by the comments of several construction workers eager to explain their handiwork, and an inspection of the interior renderings donated by a local San Diego architect, they talked for almost two hours.

By the time Mick Everett left the center just before noon, Jade felt the euphoria of having just touched the sky with her fingertips. The feature story, tentatively scheduled to appear in the paper sometime that week, would be a perfect prelude, Jade realized, to the reopening of the Activity Center.

It was also clear to her, as it would be to his readers, that Mick Everett empathized with her goals for the children. He took his empathy a step farther when he made out a personal check for the center, which he pressed into Jade's hands with endearing awkwardness.

Bursting with energy and optimism, Jade skipped lunch and spent the afternoon assembling the last of the press kits for the local TV and radio stations, a project she'd been working on for several weeks when time permitted. With less than a month to go before the Activity Center's reopening, she had her work cut out for her. But with a little luck and the kindness and generosity of the local community, she felt hopeful that the funding necessary to operate the center would be forthcoming.

Reed left the warehouse and walked down the long hallway that led to Jade's office. When he heard the sound of voices, he slowed his pace. What he saw made him pause outside the doorway.

"I like your hair," said the little girl.

Reed guessed she was six or seven. He watched Jade smooth a ragged fringe of bangs out of the child's eyes.

"I might be able to manage the same style for you if you want me to try."

The child considered her offer for a moment. "I'd have to get permission first."

"Well, when you do, Kelly, just let me know. We'll have our own hairdressing party." Still on her knees while the little girl sat on the edge of a folding chair, Jade reached for a bandage from the first-aid box on her desk.

"Is it gonna hurt again?"

"Nah. The worst part's over."

Kelly leaned forward and pursed her lips in a contemplative manner as she studied her knee. "I don't like that red stuff. It stings."

"No more red stuff then. Scout's honor." Jade gently placed the adhesive strip over Kelly's scraped knee. "There! You're as good as new. When this gets dirty or falls off, come back and I'll put a new one on for you."

"Okay." Kelly slid off the folding chair, clutching an old doll that had seen better days. "Thanks."

"You're welcome."

"You're nice," she announced with a grin that revealed two missing front teeth.

Jade sat back on her heels. "I think you're very nice, too. I guess that means we might get to be friends."

Kelly nodded, and still clutching her battered doll, flung herself into Jade's arms. The gesture was so spontaneous that Jade nearly tumbled onto the floor.

"I gotta go now," the child announced after a quick hug. "Aunt Jean might worry if she can't find me."

Jade slowly drew back. She knew the truth, of course, but she remained silent. Jean Higgins had four children of her own. Kelly was just another mouth to feed for the unemployed woman. Reaching for a peppermint stick from the jar at the edge of her desk, Jade continued to hold Kelly in a loose embrace with one arm around her narrow shoulders. "Promise me something, sweetheart."

"Anything," vowed the little girl as she reached out. With a look of satisfaction on her face, she trailed her fingers down the side of Jade's sleek fall of dark hair.

Jade slipped the cellophane off the peppermint stick and gave her the candy. Quickly choking back the emotion that had settled in her throat, she widened her eyes so that the tears filling them wouldn't spill down her cheeks and give her away. Kelly resembled someone so familiar to her that she ached deep inside.

"Be very careful walking back to the shelter, Kelly."

"Oh, I *am* careful," she answered in an amazingly solemn manner. "And I always cross to the other side of the street if I see somebody sleeping on the sidewalk."

Reed's heart clenched inside his chest. It killed him that a child so small had to be cautious about the derelicts passed out on the sidewalks in the middle of the day. He'd seen them, too, of course, and given the center's location he knew he shouldn't be surprised. Still, he hated any corruption of innocence.

"Good girl," Jade managed as Kelly dashed out of the office with a shouted "See ya!" flung over her shoulder.

She didn't get up for a moment. She didn't have the strength to move. Her tears finally fell, and she angrily scrubbed them away. Crying over children like Kelly wouldn't do them any good. Only hard work would make a difference. She exhaled heavily and got to her feet, turning in surprise when she heard Reed's voice.

"You should have children of your own."

She smiled weakly. "Kind of hard to do without a husband."

He arched an eyebrow, the necessity of words completely eliminated by his sardonic expression.

"You know what I mean," she reminded him.

He remained in the doorway, his shoulder resting against the door frame. "Yeah, I guess I do."

"Did you need something?"

"Not really." He couldn't rid his mind of the image of Jade on her knees, Kelly clasped in her arms. A raven-haired Madonna and child. "You looked good with the little one."

Her expression softened. "She's a sweet child."

"She shouldn't be in the warehouse, though. It's dangerous for her."

"You're right, but she assured me that she was careful. She apparently snuck in the back way after she made sure no one would see her."

Reed straightened and moved forward into the room. Jade was forced to lift her gaze as he came toward her. He reached out. She froze, dragged air into her lungs and then held her breath. He placed his fingertips within an inch of her shoulder, but he didn't actually touch her.

"You've got a pint-size handprint on your blouse."

She stepped back. His hand fell away. His insides tightened, but he kept his expression neutral. Even he had his pride. When Jade shied away from him or avoided his touch, it hurt him.

"It'll wash out."

"It might not."

She shrugged, puzzled by his preoccupation with the condition of her blouse.

"Maybe you should change."

She shook her head and sent her hair into a gentle swing below her chin. "No clothes."

He frowned and glanced over her shoulder at the battered locker standing in the far corner of the room. He knew she kept a change of clothes in there.

"I took everything home last night to add to my laundry basket."

He returned his gaze to her face and focused on the movement of her lips as she spoke. His control slipped. His attention wavered. He didn't really hear her last comment.

"You have a beautiful mouth. It's shaped like a bow."

"So do you," she whispered spontaneously.

"Why were you crying before?"

A nearly sleepless night of conflict and mixed emotions, a morning of renewed hope, and a visit to her past, thanks to Kelly, encouraged her frankness. "She reminds me of myself at that age."

"How so?"

"Her parents are dead. She's with her mother's sister now, but she's an afterthought most of the time. Her aunt has four children of her own, and they naturally come first." Jade sighed, closed her eyes for a long moment and pressed her fingertips to her temples. "She even looks like I did at that age. Too skinny, scraped knees, an awful haircut, infrequent baths, lonely eyes and a brave front. It hurts to see her that way. It hurts to remember myself that way."

Her revealing remark surprised him. "The family's homeless?"

"Yes. They're staying at the shelter a few blocks down the street."

He couldn't stop staring at her mouth. "Have they been there long?"

"About six months." Jade felt her tears return. "Kelly..." Her voice cracked. Finally, she managed, "She's like me. Afraid to trust."

That got his complete attention. He proceeded with great care. "She seems to trust you."

"That's just started to happen. It's taken her months."

"She's coming around, then?"

Jade nodded. "Slow but sure."

"Just like you," he observed.

Her eyes widened. "I don't know about that."

"Are you still upset?"

She flashed a brilliant and determined smile in his direction. "Not really."

He reached out again and took her hand. She didn't pull away this time. Her ability to resist him was gone. It had seeped out of her the night before, leaving her adrift in the wake of her own bewilderment. She felt a warm tingle work its way into the core of her soul when he ran his blunt fingers back and forth across the top of her hand.

"Tell me the truth, Jade."

"I'm fine, really."

"Don't lie, sweet lady."

"I'm not..."

"You're very pale."

She jerked her hand free. "I didn't have time for a tan this summer," she snapped.

"Tell me what you're feeling," he encouraged, ignoring her show of temper.

The air rushed out of her. She felt oddly deflated. What was he trying to do? Send her into a state of total witlessness?

"I...I wouldn't even know where to start."

"Why not?" he asked softly.

"A lot's happening right now," she answered vaguely. The news of Mick Everett's planned feature on the center disappeared from her thoughts like a fleeing thief.

He moved his hand up and down her arm in a motion that was slow and deliberate, soothing and seductive.

"Why are you touching me like this?"

"I want you."

"I know that, but why now?"

"Because you need me."

She shook her head, denial automatic.

Reed stopped her from saying that she didn't need anyone by moving even closer and lifting his free hand to the side of her face. He stroked her cheek with gentle finger-tips. "Don't lie. There's no need any longer."

"What do you mean?"

"I mean I won't push you. You know what I want. It's up to you now. You can call the shots."

She leaped to his defense, startling herself. "You didn't push that hard before."

He smiled, clearly not believing her.

"You didn't. I've been pushed much harder by experts. I can handle it," she insisted, her words ringing with false bravado.

"Does that mean you don't mind if I push you a little more?"

"It means..." Confused, she admitted, "I don't know what it means."

His body flashed a warning sign to him. "I won't stop wanting you."

"I think I've known that all along. I just can't figure out why."

The hand drifting up her arm moved slowly across her shoulder and down to the open vee of her blouse, but he didn't let himself actually touch her. Instead, he held his fingertips a scant inch above her flesh. "Your skin is like a furnace, and your heart's beating as though it wants to fly out of your body."

Her breath jerked in and out of her lungs in sharp pants. "You make me feel..." She looked at him helplessly. "I don't even know what words to use. I've never reacted this way to a man before."

Distracted by the increased pace of Jade's heart and the warmth emanating from her skin, he absently asked her, "Never?"

"Never."

She wished he would touch her. She wished he would peel her blouse from her body, discard her bra and fill his hands with the heat and weight of her breasts. She wanted the abrasive stubble of his face rubbing against the warmth of her sensitive skin. She wanted the feel of him sucking her flesh into his mouth. She wanted to know the stabbing forays of his tongue, and she would happily have died for what she was certain would be the torturous pleasure of him teething her nipples into an aroused state.

God! How she *wanted*!

Stunned by her thoughts, Jade stared at Reed. It didn't seem possible that he wasn't even touching her. She felt naked, vulnerable and marked by the curse of her own reckless desire as she swayed on unsteady legs.

With amazing clarity, she also knew what she didn't want any longer. She didn't want to feel like a prize left unclaimed.

"Why me?" he probed. "And why now?"

"I don't know!" she exclaimed, startled by his question. "I wish I did."

"Amazing, isn't it?"

She knew exactly what he meant, but her ability to speak abandoned her like a lost cause. Who could possibly explain what had ignited the chemistry between them? And who could explain what sustained it? She certainly couldn't.

"You aren't even sure if you like me," he challenged.

"That's not true," she gasped, the temperature of her blood rising several degrees with each passing second. She throbbed inside from the torment of being so close to him. "I like you more than I should. I always have."

Her admission arced along his nerve endings, bringing with it a physical response that made the muscles of his thighs quiver. "When I held you the other night, you trembled in my arms. Your skin was hot then, too, and you re-

minded me of honey bubbling in the center of a giant flame.
I wanted to feel you melt all over me, and then I wanted to
absorb you into my skin. I still do.''

She flushed, aroused and embarrassed by the darkness,
the danger, the effortless seduction in his voice. But his gaze
was so compelling that she couldn't make herself look away.
Unconsciously she rubbed her cheek against his palm.

His hand tingled, but he made himself continue. ''I
thought it was the most beautiful thing in the world. Your
trembling, I mean.''

She found herself hanging on to each softly whispered
and erotically suggestive word that passed his lips. ''I don't
know what to say.''

The tension of holding his hand next to her heated skin
and not touching her took its toll. His fingers shook. The
muscles in his arm and shoulders bunched and jumped with
restraint. His eyes seemed even darker than usual.

Reed reluctantly lowered his aching arm to his side, but
he didn't remove his other hand from her cheek. If he got
too close to her, he cautioned himself, or if he put his hand
on any other part of her body, he knew he would lose the
final thread of what had become unstable control. For the
moment, the torture of simply being near her would suf-
fice.

''Why do you have to say anything?'' he asked.

Jade fell silent, mesmerized by the blatant hunger reflected in his eyes. She exhaled shakily.

''Your nipples felt like little daggers when we danced. It
was almost like having you naked in my arms.''

She moaned, the sound coming from deep inside. ''Don't,
please.''

He ignored her. ''They got so hard so fast,'' he mused
almost to himself, his voice low and filled with wonder.

"So did you," she whispered without a thought to the impropriety of the remark. They'd long since shifted to another dimension, a dimension lacking in reality to such an extent that none of the rules of convention seemed to apply.

He smiled—that predatory smile of his which could inspire fear and should definitely inspire caution. "I don't have to be dancing with you to have that happen. All I have to do is think about you. No woman has ever..."

"Has ever what?" she pressed when he hesitated.

"I've never had a woman who could turn the flame up so high, so quickly."

"Does that bother you?" she asked, feeling utterly brazen.

He released the pent-up air burning his lungs through gritted teeth, the thin high sound emerging like an animal's warning against anyone intruding on its personal terrain. "Lady, you risk a lot with me."

"You're always saying that."

"It's the truth."

"I believe you, but I know what I'm doing." Her chin came up and the expression on her face challenged him to call her a liar.

"I wonder."

"I'm not innocent."

"Maybe. Maybe not," he replied quietly.

She faltered. She certainly didn't want him to think her a total babe in the woods. "I was involved with someone after college. He left me for a better job."

"Fool!" The single word held a wealth of contempt.

"He didn't think so."

"He didn't think, period."

"Thank you," she breathed.

"For what? The truth?"

"No. For always making me feel so . . ."

"Desirable, wanted, needed?" he supplied easily.

She nodded, her expression troubled, innocent and gloriously evocative all at the same time. "You make me feel like a woman."

He smiled again, but it was only a quick upturn of the corners of his mouth. She would have missed it if her gaze hadn't been riveted on the hard planes of his face.

"I haven't yet, but I'd like to."

She sighed audibly. "I think I'd like that, too."

Something inside him shattered. His heart felt like a lurching pump in his chest, and a surge of sweet hot desire scalded his bloodstream. "Why, Jade?"

"Because I'm tired of fighting. I'm tired of denying myself. And because I . . . want you."

"You . . . want . . . *me*?" he asked, slowly and distinctly.

"I want you."

"You want me to touch you?"

"Yes." The word slipped from her like a whisper.

"You want me to strip the clothes from your body and touch you with my hands and my mouth?"

She trembled. "Yes."

"You want me inside of you, making love with you?"

"Oh, God!"

"Tell me," he insisted, almost ruthless in his intensity.

Reed desperately wanted to drag her into his arms, but he didn't let himself. This moment was so intense and erotic that he was loath to disturb it. The touching would come later. At least he prayed it would. Unless, of course, she changed her mind.

"I want you . . . that way."

"Say the words," he urged as he towered over her.

She suddenly couldn't see anything but his taut features and broad shoulders. He blocked out the world. He also

blocked her path to the door. She hesitated, suddenly uncertain and frightened of what was happening between
them. "Why?"

"Because I need to hear them. And I want to make sure
you're going into this with your eyes wide open."

Shocked, she tilted her head to one side as she peered up
at him. The movement sent a cascade of silken hair across
the back of his hand. "You don't trust me to know my own
mind?"

He forced himself to lower his hand from her cheek. Ex-
haling raggedly, he also gave in to the urging of his conscience, that part of him that was intent on protecting her
despite the cost to himself. "I think you've been under a lot
of pressure lately—a lot of it from me."

The rules to this bizarre game had just shifted, she realized. Her voice deceptively soft, Jade asked, "Are you
trying to talk me out of making love with you?" She didn't
bother to wait for a reply. "You've changed the rules every
time it's suited you, Reed. I'm not going to let you do it
again."

He drew in a sharp breath, his body on the verge of deto-
nation. He sensed the subtle change that had just taken
place within her. And he sensed her certainty about what
would happen between them. It shouldn't have shocked
him, he knew, but it did. It took him a few moments to realize that he hadn't planned on her willingness.

She gave him an openly assessing look. "I want us to
make love, not just have sex together. I want to feel you inside me. Now, do you believe me?" she asked softly.

He opened his mouth and formed a single word with his
lips, but he couldn't make his voice work. Bested, he
conceded with a nod.

"What happens next, Reed?"

He finally answered her, but the words resembled a full clip of bullets being fired from a .45 automatic at close range. "Come home with me. We'll have dinner. Whatever happens, happens."

"Tonight?" she questioned, ignoring his terseness.

He nodded again, his hands now clenched at his sides.

"Around five?"

He nodded a third time, much to his chagrin. Jade was full of surprises. He made himself a promise that he wouldn't let her surprise him again, at least not in the next ten minutes.

She felt strangely buoyed by his silence, his sudden lack of macho confidence. "Where do you live?"

"Del Mar."

Delight sparkled in her eyes. "On the beach?"

He smiled—a very smug smile that Jade didn't quite understand.

"Could we take a walk while the sun sets?"

"If you'd like."

"I'd love it."

Love *me*, he thought spontaneously. Feeling as though someone had just dropped a rock on his head, Reed sobered. Where had that come from? he wondered, his expression stark.

"When it finally happens between us, Jade, it's going to be like dynamite exploding."

Her eyes widened, her thick dark lashes unable to obscure her surprise. She felt a quiver start deep inside her. "I think I've known that all along. It frightened me before, but for some reason it doesn't any longer. I do wonder, though, if I'll survive it."

He took a step backward, and then another, not at all puzzled by her final comment. Fear seemed to be at the root of the battles they'd waged and would likely continue to wage. But she was right. Survival was a crucial issue, one they would both have to confront.

He knew he couldn't let himself forget that she would eventually move on to someone more appropriate for her, but he ruthlessly shoved that painful reality aside. He'd already faced the fact that he would never measure up to her standards in a man because of his lack of education and polish. For now, he told himself, he would take what she was willing to offer. He would deal with the aftermath of their love affair only when it arrived.

"Later, sweet lady," he said in a rough voice.

She smiled—a tremulous quirking of her lips that nearly drove him right back to her side. "Later," she echoed as he turned and strode out the door.

Jade, awash in an incredible array of emotions, made her way to the chair behind her desk like a shaken accident victim. She couldn't stop marveling over the fact that Reed had barely touched her, and yet she felt well and truly seduced by what had just taken place between them.

Although she tried to finish the press kits stacked on her desk, she soon gave up the pretense of work. Jade couldn't ignore the thoughts racing through her mind, any more than she could ignore the events she'd just set in motion by agreeing to spend the evening with Reed.

He wanted her. She knew that. His desire had been clear since the very start. But how long would it last? she wondered. It was an unanswerable question at the moment, she realized.

Only time would reveal Reed's intentions and motives, aside from the obvious one. Just the thought of risking herself and her emotions unnerved her, but she knew it was time to try. More important, she wanted to hope again. She needed that ability restored to her after having gone so many years without it.

Unwilling to run from the truth of her actions, she logically considered the reasons for her change of heart. As a result, she simply continued a process that had begun the night before.

Honesty and integrity forced her to accept her feelings for Reed. He intrigued her, he maddened her, and he enthralled her, in person and in her fantasies. He made her hungry, he made her feel, really *feel*, and he made her heart weep for want of his love.

Dynamic, forceful and compelling in both personality and manner, he possessed an unending list of qualities she admired. Attractive, sensual and incredibly earthy, he also made her entire being ache at the mere sight of him.

In truth, there really wasn't anything about him that she didn't appreciate. His macho behavior, something right out of the eighteenth century, appealed to her even when he blatantly exercised his old-fashioned belief that a woman should be looked after.

She didn't question his desire for her, either. It was constantly there, pulsing with life and just as vital as her desire for him. He'd dismantled the walls around her heart with amazing skill, and he had forced her to confront the feelings buried deep inside. Although she'd frequently cursed his nerve, she now blessed his determination.

She had never before experienced the intense, almost primitive need he inspired, not even with Mark, her only lover. She wouldn't ever forget how hurt she had been after he'd casually strolled out of her life.

She had given Mark two precious gifts; her trust, which he'd carelessly discarded, and her virginity, which apparently was of even less value to him than her faith in him. It had taken her a long time to understand that he was nothing but a selfish man intent on pursuing his own personal agenda. In the final analysis, her needs and her emotional well-being hadn't ever been a consideration in their short-lived relationship.

Reed returned to the forefront of her mind, swiftly displacing her melancholy memories. She was falling in love with him. That realization, for some inexplicable reason, didn't even shock her.

Perhaps it was the combination of two months of sizzling awareness and a series of sleepless nights like the one she'd just spent—nights that had finally forced her to confront the singularity and loneliness of her existence. Or maybe Kelly, as much a victim of disinterest as she herself had been, had helped her to understand that it wasn't necessary or desirable to remain isolated forever.

Whatever the reasons, she'd walked to the edge of her world and viewed the lonely years ahead. Her dread of being alone indefinitely, a keen hunger for intimacy and warmth, and the dream of a safe harbor in the arms of a man she cared for combined to form an undeniable truth! She *needed* to reach out, she *wanted* to reach out—even though the very idea of exposing herself to rejection or abandonment still frightened her.

And she wanted Reed Townsend. She would have him, perhaps not forever, but at least for a while. The choice was simple. She could remain bound by her fears and trapped forever by the past, or she could seize this chance to feel whole as a woman. Whatever the risks involved, she would knowingly take them, but she would also remain wise and not give away her true feelings for him. Her pride required at least that much of her.

She wouldn't turn back now, nor would she deny the fates. She'd reached a turning point, perhaps even a point of no return as far as her heart was concerned. And if caring for Reed made her more vulnerable, she consciously accepted that possibility as an unstated condition of their relationship.

She did wonder, of course, if she would ever know what was in his heart, but she cautioned herself not to expect anything more of him than his desire. She sensed that Reed would give as much as he would take in the sensual arena, but the facts he'd revealed about his past left her with the feeling that he hated the idea of vulnerability in himself. She couldn't blame him for feeling self-protective, not with an unfaithful wife and a father he apparently hated as part of his personal emotional baggage.

She smiled just thinking about him. He reminded her of a tornado with that volatile temper of his. She grasped too, with unexpected clarity, the all-encompassing scope of her own emotions. Although unnerved by the depth and texture of her feelings for Reed, she promised herself that she wouldn't behave like a coward about her needs ever again.

Jade glanced up in surprise when she heard the sound of approaching footsteps. His measured tread was as familiar to her as an old friend.

"Later" had just arrived, and much more quickly than she'd expected. Her heart raced, forcing her to take a steadying breath. She watched the doorway and held her breath as Reed stepped into view.

"Sorry I'm late. I had a problem at the office."

Jade only half heard him. No longer dressed in his normal construction garb of work boots, dungarees and T-shirt, he appeared freshly showered and newly shaved. He wore a pair of dress slacks and a pin-striped shirt with a button-down collar, the cuffs rolled up to reveal the dense tawny hair on his muscular arms. His hair, still damp, looked as though he'd run his fingers through it in a hurried effort to tame it into place. She stared at him, totally unprepared for the surge of hunger that swept over her.

"Did you hear what I said, Jade?"

She jerked herself free of her miring thoughts. "Oh, yes, of course. I didn't mind." She waved at the stack of folders on her desk. "I've had plenty to do."

"Ready to go, or do you need a little more time?"

It was now or never, she realized. She reached for her purse and flashed a bright smile at him. "I just have to lock up."

"Everything's taken care of except the back door," he told her.

It was obvious that he was in a hurry. She lagged a little as she rounded the edge of her desk, a frown settling across her forehead.

"Jade?"

"Yes?" she asked with another nervous show of teeth.

Reed grimaced when he saw her strained smile. "This isn't an execution, you know. And nothing's going to happen unless you're ready for it."

She exhaled heavily, managed to relax a little and produced the first genuine smile he'd seen since his arrival. He shook his head and grinned down at her, sliding his arm around her waist as he escorted her along the hallway and out the back door. "Relax, okay? I don't bite."

"Awww," she groaned almost mournfully. "And here I was hoping that you did."

He laughed, the sound echoing across the parking lot. Jade grinned up at him, feeling like a carefree imp and loving the fact that she could really be herself around him. She didn't stop to consider the fact that she wouldn't have said anything even remotely similar to any other man on the planet.

Six

―――

Less than half an hour later, Reed escorted Jade into his beachfront home. He watched her eyes widen and heard her swift intake of breath as she walked into the center of the living room.

He remained standing at the edge of the tiled foyer, his own breathing strangely erratic as he watched her react to her surroundings. She slowly turned full circle, her arms lifting as though in a welcoming embrace. The wonder and delight on her face and the sparkle in her eyes expressed her appreciation for the simple elegance of the sprawling open design of the trilevel house.

"This is spectacular," she breathed. She glanced at Reed, who stood as still and sturdy as a towering oak. She saw pride of ownership in his eyes, but she also saw much more. "You designed it and built it yourself, didn't you?"

He nodded, his pleasure at her insightfulness evident in the subdued smile that softened the angles of his face. He began to breathe more normally again.

Situated in an exclusive section of Del Mar, the house was worth an astronomical sum, but for Reed its true value would never be measured in dollars. The current market price of the house didn't really matter to him, but roots and a sense of belonging did. Somehow those two needs took on even greater significance now that Jade was here.

Jade could see that the house personified the man. It announced his environmental preferences in the unvarnished open beams of the vaulted ceiling, declared his individuality in its sprawling disregard for compartmentalization and reflected, in the sweeping design and strong burgundy and navy decor, his straightforward manner. His personal statement was further exemplified in the comfortable, masculine-style furniture, a collection of dramatic sculptures, and paintings that expressed boldness, confidence and inner strength.

She crossed the massive lower level of Reed's home, her footsteps audible on the hardwood floor. Pausing before a wide wall of glass that extended to the very top of the tri-level vaulted ceiling, she looked out across the deck to the stretch of beach and even wider expanse of ocean beyond it.

Deep blue waves surged, peaked whitely and then disappeared in continuous harmony all the way to the horizon. The compelling quality of the view reminded her of Reed.

She turned to face him, her smile both sincere and shy. "I love the beach."

"I know" almost slipped out of his mouth, but he managed to engage his brain before revealing one of Jade's preferences that only her anonymous caller would know.

Reed went to the bar, filled a wineglass with a light California Zinfandel and poured himself a bourbon on the rocks. He joined Jade and handed her the long-stemmed wineglass.

"You're very good at this, aren't you?"

"Good at what, Jade?" He took a quick slug of his drink and waited for her reply.

"Seduction," she whispered.

He grinned. "Not by a long shot."

"I'm nervous," she announced baldly, the liquid in her wineglass sloshing slightly against the rim in response to her trembling.

He exhaled, the air leaving his body in a weighted gust. "Don't feel alone."

Shocked by his comment, she looked up at him and finally comprehended his serious demeanor. "You're nervous?"

"Women haven't cornered the market on that particular emotion, you know."

"What do you have to feel nervous about?"

"You."

"I don't understand. I'm here by choice."

"You're also terrified," he noted bluntly. "That doesn't exactly inspire confidence in a man."

"Oh." She gave him a puzzled look. "I'm not really terrified, just a little edgy." Feeling every bit of the edginess she'd just confessed, Jade hurriedly sipped her wine. "This is very good."

He smiled at her attempt to divert him. "Come on over here and sit down with me."

She let him lead her to one of the two matching couches. Gingerly perching on the edge of a plump cushion, she watched in surprise as Reed kicked off his leather deck shoes and settled on an area rug that covered the floor between the sofas.

She kept her eyes on him as he tilted his head from one side to the other, rolled his shoulders back and forth a few times and then leaned back against the couch. His shoulder brushed the side of her leg and sent a shaft of heat all the way to the top of her thigh. She trembled, tightening her hold on the stem of her wineglass.

Telling herself to relax, she said, "You've had a long day, haven't you? You must be tired." She reached out with her free hand before she could stop herself, bringing her fingertips to rest on the back of his neck.

He flinched at her unexpected touch and then told himself to relax. Her hand fell away before he could follow the directive. Mindful of Jade's nervousness, he knew he couldn't pursue the urges pumping furiously through his body quite yet, so he made himself answer, even though idle conversation was the last thing on his mental priority list. "I'm not tired exactly, but it has been a hell of a day."

"Want to talk about it?"

"Maybe later."

"How about now?" she encouraged.

He gave in to the plea behind those three words. "There was an accident on a jobsite in Oceanside. Two of my men were taken to the hospital. They'll be released in the morning. They've both admitted that they got careless and ignored the safety rules I insist on, but it still bothers me when anyone gets hurt on one of my jobs. I think this heat has made everyone a little crazy and a lot sloppy."

"Feel better?"

He glanced at her and nodded, his mouth quirking in a reluctant smile. Jade leaned forward and placed her glass on the coffee table in front of the couch. Reed breathed deeply of her scent and thought, not for the first time, that the unique fragrance of her skin affected him like an aphrodisiac.

She responded to her own needs now and placed her hands on his shoulders. When Reed didn't protest or shift away, she moved her fingers rhythmically back and forth across the wide expanse of muscle and bone.

Focused on the strength and durability of his body, she nearly jumped when he stilled her hands and gently drew her from the couch. After helping her remove her shoes, he eased her onto his lap and cradled her against his chest, his breathing uneven and his thoughts in turmoil.

"You're making it almost impossible for me to be a gentleman," he muttered.

She knew he spoke the truth. Touching him had been a conscious invitation, one prompted by the primitive feelings taunting her. She lifted her head and looked him in the eye. "I don't want you to be a gentleman."

She could feel his arousal surge against her hip, and she clearly understood the reasons for the strain on his face and the pulse throbbing wildly at his temple. She also suspected that the arms around her now trembled from the tension of restraint. His sensitivity touched and warmed her heart.

He tucked her head into the curve between his neck and shoulder and simply held her, all the while trying to ignore the rampaging fire in his blood. He ran his hands up and down her spine, as though measuring her and soothing her at the same time. Every time she shifted, even just a little as she fitted herself more comfortably against him, he fought the screaming urge to bury himself deep inside her.

"Why are you really here?" he asked, his voice revealing the effort of his self-control.

"Because I want to be."

"That's not good enough, sweet lady."

She raised her head and looked at him. How could she admit that after a treacherous emotional roller-coaster ride, she'd finally accepted her feelings for him? She simply couldn't. Not yet, anyway. The risk was too great and her courage—the courage that allowed her to be with him now—was too fragile, too needful of care and nurturing.

Lifting her hand, she gently outlined his lips with the tip of one finger. She watched his lips part, and she stared in fascination as he sucked her finger into his mouth and swirled his tongue around it. She gasped, startled by the intimacy of the gesture and the searing heat that bathed her senses.

"I wouldn't be here if I didn't care about you, Reed."

He frowned. "That's all I'm gonna get, isn't it?"

She nodded, too mesmerized by the fire leaping in his eyes as he watched her and by the sensual stroking of his tongue as he shifted his attention to the open palm of her hand to question his frown or to hear the regret in his voice. Heat engulfed her, melting her nerves and smothering any mixed emotions she once might have had about becoming his lover.

"I don't want to talk anymore," she whispered.

Taut with need, he paused and reminded her, "I promised you dinner."

She shook her head, her gaze riveted on his face. "Later."

"Our walk on the beach?"

"Later," she answered softly. She lowered her hand to a button on his shirt, her fingers clumsy as she tugged it free. "You've spent the past two months trying to seduce me, Reed Townsend. Are you going to back out on me now?"

"No way, lady," he all but growled. "No way in hell."

"Then I need both of my hands." She gently freed the one he'd tantalized with his mouth. Her damp palm still tingled from those lazy swipes of his tongue.

Before he could move, she tugged open a second, a third and then a fourth button, the expression on her face as sensual as Eve's when Jade separated the fabric of his shirt and held her hands, palms flat and fingers extended, a centimeter or less above his chest.

She glanced at him, an ingenuous look on her face. "Now I need to touch you."

He held his breath as she connected with his hair-roughened skin. Shuddering at the contact, he gripped her hips with both hands, shifting under her in such a way that his groin seemed to pulsate against her. She moaned, the sound reaching inside him to reduce even more his steadily dwindling control.

Her eyes fell closed just before she sank her fingers into the dense pelt of tawny hair that covered his chest. She heard him inhale sharply and felt the shift and play of warm flesh and hard muscle beneath her fingertips. Her fingers arched of their own accord, her nails lightly scoring his skin. She realized that she could spend the next ninety years touching him, exploring him. She also knew it still wouldn't be enough.

"What are you doing?" he asked raggedly.

She opened her eyes and gave him an impertinent look, too caught up in the emotions circling her heart to be cautious or nervous any longer. "You don't know?"

He marveled at the combination of naiveté and boldness in her personality. She never ceased to surprise him. "Lady..."

"I'm tempting fate," she announced.

Reed groaned and imprisoned her face in callused hands. "Fate welcomes you."

She smiled gently. "Fate is gracious and wise."

She slipped her arms around his neck as naturally as waves embrace a shoreline—at least that was the final coherent thought Reed managed as he lowered his mouth and sampled the natural sweetness of this woman and the fruity flavor of the wine still lingering on her lips.

His kiss was a heady combination of hunger and seduction, a tantalizing hint of his prowess as a lover. Jade sank into his embrace with the abandon of a woman willingly submerging herself in quicksand. Her lips parted almost immediately, her tongue meeting his in a sudden, parrying thrust.

A great crushing weight seemed to press down on her chest, making her heart roar in her ears and her respiration so rapid that she gasped. But he caught the inarticulate sound in his mouth, tilted his head slightly to one side and thrust even deeper into the wet warmth hidden behind her lips. He stroked the delicate inner walls of her cheeks with devastating skill, traced the even line of her teeth and then circled her tongue for an endless time before sucking it into his own mouth.

Jade surged against him, pressing her breasts to the hard wall of his chest as though compelled to become a physical extension of him. She tested the taste and texture of his mouth, challenging him with the same exploratory journey he'd just taken. Clinging to him, she thought that she'd never felt so free, so filled with the limitless wonder of her emotions. And she finally understood that she had never really loved before.

Without releasing her mouth, Reed worked Jade's skirt up to her hips and then shifted her so that she straddled him. He ran his hands up and down her thighs, kneading the resilient silkiness of her skin with the constrained force of his blunt fingers while he probed the recesses of her mouth. His reach extended to her hips and his hands were strikingly possessive as he cupped her bottom and brought her even closer to his body.

It seemed as if something almost dangerous lurked inside him as he held her, and he knew that the possessiveness he felt for Jade would be a part of him for as long as he lived.

But so was the hurtful realization that he had no right to stake his claim on her heart. He couldn't meet the standards she deserved in a man, and he would never accept her loving him out of pity. His hands tightened on her and his mouth grew momentarily harsh as he fought the anguish of his thoughts.

Jade felt the change in him and responded to it, hungry and desperate for more of him. She whimpered in protest when he relinquished her swollen lips, and she sighed raggedly when his mouth lightly grazed her cheek.

Moving slowly, he savored the fragrances and softness of her skin—skin so soft, so unlike anything he had ever felt before. He paused suddenly and lifted his head, his eyes filled with darkly flaring sensual intent.

Too overcome to do anything else, Jade simply stared back at him as the seconds ticked by. Her face grew flushed, her lips remained wet from his kisses and her eyes, feverish and dazed with need, widened briefly and then fluttered closed. She felt utterly sapped of strength and will.

"It's my turn to tempt fate," he whispered hoarsely.

Unable to form a reply, Jade eased back a few inches, clasped his hands and lifted them to the level of her breasts.

She sensed what he wanted. She *knew* what she needed.

She'd known for weeks now, even if she hadn't been willing to accept that Reed's possession of her was inevitable, if only to appease the ache in her soul and the emptiness in her life. The aching emptiness in her heart would have to wait for satisfaction, because she couldn't make her emotional needs his responsibility.

Her eyes appeared glazed and her breathing took on an irregular cadence. She pressed his open palms against the swollen mounds of her breasts, which were too achy and too needy to survive any longer without his hands on them. Her nipples, already ultrasensitive, hardened instantly.

Reed felt the swift change in her body despite the barrier
of her blouse and bra. He closed his eyes on a groan and
pressed his hands flush against her upper body. The contact devastated him. Fierce hunger kicked in again, bringing with it a surge of heat and strength to his groin.

Jade felt the increased pressure and moved sinuously atop
him. She pushed herself down, the desperate ache inside her
growing more and more pronounced with every gasping
breath she took.

"Touch me," she begged, too immersed now in the tu-
multuous storm raging inside her to care about maintaining
her dignity or her emotional distance. Love and passion, she
fleetingly realized, stripped the soul to the barest essentials.

He released the buttons of her blouse and the clasp of her
bra, sweeping both from her body in a matter of seconds. At
first he couldn't do anything but stare at the exquisite beauty
of her. Reaching out, he cupped the weight of her firm
breasts, his eyes fixed on her pink nipples, which seemed
destined to remind him forever of delicate little daggers.

Jade drew in enough air to sustain her body and arched
her back in blatant invitation as she pressed herself into his
hands. She quivered at his touch and a fine mist of perspiration covered her skin while he played her like a master.

She felt his breath, hot and damp, sigh across her skin as
he made his way down the side of her neck with his lips and
across the fragile bones at the base of her throat. She savored his skill and talent as he stroked her trembling flesh,
unaware that he was trembling, too—a sudden and nearly
shattering kind of trembling in the region of his heart.

He massaged her breasts, his touch utterly torturous each
time he strayed to her peaked nipples. Her skin scorched his
palms and his fingers, marking him, claiming him, driving
him higher and higher even as he repeatedly drove her closer
and closer to the edge of insanity.

This time is for Jade, he told himself. This time would be hers alone, but the breathtaking beauty of the woman and the moment would be his to behold and to remember.

Her struggle became more profound, almost painfully intense. "Reed?"

"What, sweet lady?"

"Help me. I don't know..."

Her broken plea became a gasp of shock when he shifted her forward. He drew her breast into his mouth, his tongue swirling around her distended nipple, his teeth nipping gently, as he pressed her hips against the ridge of flesh at the base of his torso. He felt her begin to writhe and he understood, even encouraged, her quest.

She was like a blazing inferno in his arms, the flames scorching his hands and his soul. No more ice. No more control. She seemed to have abandoned every self-protective instinct she possessed.

He felt awed by her innate sensuality. He marveled at her frankness about her needs. He treasured her trust. And he finally understood that the circumstances of her past had forced her to deny parts of herself that were essential to her identity.

Her journey seemed endless, her quest uncertain. Jade felt wild, untamed, even insatiable. Caught in a turbulent inner storm, she held tightly to Reed and twisted and arched and drove herself forward in search of something she didn't understand. She grew frantic. She pushed even harder, grinding herself into him until she teetered on the brink of an abyss that suddenly terrified her.

Reed sensed how close she was and that she was fighting herself. He forced her more snugly against his throbbing body, a body so close to flash point that he almost abandoned his shaky control. He guided her hips until she moved instinctively again, then returned his mouth to her breasts.

The forceful suckling spewed heat into her bloodstream and flung a shaft of sensitivity directly into the pulsing center of her desire.

"I need you," she cried, her eyes tightly closed, her fingernails digging into his shoulders and her body so rigid that Reed feared that she might break apart in his arms.

"Let go, Jade. I'm here for you. Don't fight me." He surged up against her and heard the wild cry that escaped her lips.

Tension coiled even more tightly inside her, scattering her wits to the four winds. Her movements became sharp, nearly frenzied, and her breathing, a series of great gasping sounds.

Reed knew her destiny. He knew, too, that he was her guide, her protector. For now, that was enough.

"Let go, Jade," he urged. "Let go and trust me."

His words were like a trigger. When the spasms began, she fell victim to the power jolting through her and the intense inner tremors that seemed to go on forever.

Devastated, shattered and breathing unevenly, she cried out again and again and tumbled into an endless free-fall of intense sensation that bordered on pain. With tears streaming down her cheeks, she tremored repeatedly before slumping against Reed.

He held her securely, the air rasping in and out of his lungs as his heart pounded in accelerated counterpoint to the woman draped, breathless and seemingly boneless, across his broad chest. She regained herself slowly, aware that Reed was gently stroking her back and shoulders.

She felt damp all over and drained, and her body still throbbed and tingled, although with far less force. The feeling reminded her of mild convulsions receding in ever-widening circular waves, and the achiness in the lower regions of her body no longer frightened her.

And although she felt depleted, she also felt reborn.

"I think I died," she finally breathed against his neck a long while later.

He chuckled softly. "So the French claim."

She tried to lift her head from his shoulder, but the attempt proved futile. "I can't move."

He wrapped his arms more tightly around her. "There's no need."

She remained silent for a while. Reed was content to hold her until he felt the sudden trembling in her body. He lifted her away from him and saw the tears shimmering in her eyes. He sensed what might be bothering her.

"Don't be embarrassed."

"I'm not!" she exclaimed.

"Then what's wrong?"

"I wanted..." She hesitated, unsure how to voice what she felt compelled to say.

"You wanted what?" He watched her, his expression tender as he continued to run his hands up and down her arms and across her shoulders.

She reached down between them and placed her fingertips on the strained fabric that covered the undiminished strength and power of him. When he jumped, she knew she was somehow in the wrong. "I feel selfish. I want to satisfy you, too."

"You will."

She flushed, and he cursed his own rough bluntness. She nodded finally, her gaze skittering off to a point somewhere beyond his right shoulder.

She sagged into him again and buried her face against his throat. "I feel like a twit, getting ahead of myself that way."

"I wanted to watch you fly apart in my arms."

Emotionally raw, she jerked upright and demanded, "You planned this?"

He shrugged. "Actually, it just kind of happened."

"Did I pass your test?" she snapped, embarrassed that she seemed to have become some kind of event for him to watch.

Reed gripped her arms and studied her through narrowed eyes. She resembled a disheveled rag doll and his heart ached for the vulnerability he glimpsed in her eyes. He gentled his hold and forced himself to relax.

"I don't give grades, so there's no damned reason to feel awkward. Anything that happens between us is private and very precious to me. Haven't you figured that out yet?"

Her lower lip trembled, and her tears splashed across her cheeks. "I guess I'm still nervous."

"Why?"

"Because, as I've so aptly demonstrated, I don't know the first thing about bedroom etiquette."

"This is the living room," he reminded her in a perfectly level voice, but humor danced in his eyes.

It took her a second or two, but she soon put the words and the light in his eyes together and made sense of his mood. She playfully whacked his shoulder and started to laugh, too.

"You were extraordinary," he told her.

Her laughter stopped abruptly and wedged in her throat.

"And the sounds you make are enough to drive a man out of his skull."

"Reed!"

"Your skin gets all damp, and there's a pink flush in your cheeks and you throw your head back and sink your teeth into your lower lip just before it happens. It's really incredible."

"*It's* never happened to me before," she whispered, her voice and her expression starkly vulnerable.

He grasped her chin and lifted her face. "Never?"

She met his gaze without flinching. "No." She was shocked to see a glimmer of supremely male pride in his eyes. "Now, don't get all macho on me."

"Didn't he care enough to help you?"

She shrugged. Oddly, the memory no longer hurt. "He didn't care at all. It took me a long time to understand that his personal agenda didn't include anyone else's needs."

Disbelief etched Reed's face. "But you're so responsive. He was a damned fool."

"You've said that before," she noted aloud, amazed and fascinated by some of the things he said to her.

"I meant it then, and I mean it now." He tugged her forward so that her breasts plumped against his chest. His eyes fell closed and the air in his lungs escaped noisily.

Jade looped her arms around his neck and snugged into him, swaying slightly back and forth in his arms. She heard Reed's faint groan and moved again.

"You like that, don't you?" she asked when his embrace tightened. She felt oddly powerful and exulted in the feeling.

"Yes, sweet lady, I like that. But if you tease me, be prepared to pay the piper."

Jade smiled and pressed her lips to the corded muscles along the side of his neck. Reed trembled beneath her. She moved her hips experimentally and delighted in the surging pressure of his arousal. His arms tightened even more, but she was too entranced by the headiness of her own actions to worry over dented ribs.

She also knew that Reed wouldn't ever knowingly hurt her. He was simply responding to her. She let herself wish for a moment that he could love her, too; but she knew better than to wish for the moon for very long. It was firmly fixed in the night sky, just as she was firmly fixed to the realities of terra firma.

Jade felt protected by the setting sun and the shadows that had begun to fall across the room. She also felt the steadiness of Reed's protectiveness. While he might tease her, even fight toe-to-toe with her, she sensed he wouldn't ever ridicule her or her lack of experience. She knew it wasn't in him to be cruel or careless with another person's feelings.

"I want to feel you in—" she blithely began.

Reed jerked her into a more accessible position and clamped his mouth down over hers before she could complete the sentence. Another word, the merest hint of what he craved tumbling past her lips, and she would send him over the edge.

That breathless voice of hers was more erotic than anything he'd ever heard. Volatility seethed inside him, and he struggled for control even as she sucked his tongue into her mouth and teased and tormented his senses.

Half innocent, half wanton, she continued to amaze and entice him. He could feel her coming alive in his arms again. The tremors running through her tested his control. The soft sounds emerging from the back of her throat repeatedly drove him to the brink.

At the rate they were going, he would end up taking her on the floor—something he didn't want to do. Reed reluctantly separated their straining mouths, removed her from his lap and placed her on the floor next to him.

She sat there, clad only in her scrunched-up skirt. She struggled to get her breath as her breasts, the nipples taut and inviting, heaved with the strain of drawing air in and out of her body.

One glance at her wide eyes and flushed face forced Reed to his feet. He tugged her up beside him and swept her into his arms. He didn't speak as he took the stairs two at a time to the second level of his home and strode into his spacious bedroom. She slid from his arms and stood beside the bed.

Jade was cognizant of nothing but Reed, the desire that harshened his face, and the exotic play of muscles across his broad chest as he shed his shirt and reached for his belt buckle. She stared at him and then glanced at the bed, an endless expanse covered in dark silk. A low wave of apprehension washed across her confidence.

Reed, alert to her hesitation, paused. "Are you all right?"

She sank to the edge of the bed before answering. "Just kind of tied up in knots."

He tugged his belt free and dropped it on a chair nearby, his eyes fixed on her with a burning kind of intensity.

"And hungry," she admitted.

His gut clenched.

"Hungry for you," she clarified, extending her hand. She loved it that he stepped forward immediately and caught her fingers securely in his own. He seemed to understand her need for reassurance. "I'm ready, and I'm protected."

He nodded, too startled to say anything. Her surprises never ceased. He had been prepared to protect her, only to find that she'd already dealt with the issue herself.

Somewhat bemused by how frequently she turned the tables on him, he pressed a hot kiss into the palm of her hand and than watched her reach for the zipper at the side of her skirt. He stared in rapt fascination as her breasts flowed in concert with the shifting of her graceful body. She shimmied the skirt down her hips and stepped out of it.

Reed inhaled sharply when he saw the red panties she wore, which clung like a skimpy string bikini to the flaring width of her hips. He knew she would be wet from before, and the thought made his senses spark with sharp awareness.

Grateful for the semidarkness of the room, Jade watched him discard the rest of his clothing. He moved toward her, big and powerful and gloriously male. "You can stop this any time you feel the need, Jade. I'll understand."

She barely heard him as she flowed into his arms. She didn't want anything to stop what they were about to share. She felt as though she'd waited for him all her life. His sex jutted between them, stroking her, marking her, branding her as his as she fitted herself against him.

"This is about as brazen as I get. You'll have to help me the rest of the way."

He grinned. "With pleasure."

She frowned up at him. "You don't have to sound so experienced, you know."

"Jealous?"

"Of what?"

"All the women in my past?"

She gave him a severe look. "Totally!"

He laughed, swung her up into his arms and quite literally took her breath away as he whisked her onto the center of the bed. Dropping to a spot beside her, Reed lowered his hand to her belly and felt the slight trembling of muscles beneath the skin stretched taut across her abdomen.

"You just can't be like any other woman, can you?"

She froze and started to retreat from his touch.

He held her still, puzzled by her reaction. "I meant that as a compliment."

When she didn't say anything, he pulled her flush against him, his hand like an anchor on her hip. "You say what's on your mind. I've never known anyone like you. You're always surprising me."

"Do you hate it?" she asked in a small voice. She'd been different all her life, and the net result had been isolation and loneliness.

He lowered his lips to her forehead after smoothing back her bangs. "How in God's name could I hate your honesty? Your openness is part of what makes you so special."

She weighed his words and decided to trust him.

When she met his gaze, Reed saw the acceptance of his comment in her eyes. He savored her mouth with aching tenderness as he stroked her from hip to breasts. Jade trembled in his arms and clung to him, her tongue twining erotically with his.

She smoothed her fingertips across the hard flesh of his shoulders as she turned into him, offering herself in the only way she knew how. Her skin, already responsive, grew more and more sensitive as he touched her.

She felt the same crushing pressure that she'd experienced the first time, but now it didn't frighten her. She welcomed the breathlessness, the roaring in her ears. She embraced the feeling of being cast upon the turbulent waters of a storm-battered ocean, just as she embraced the power and passion of the man causing the storm that played havoc with her body and her senses.

Reed licked circles around one nipple and then the other. He journeyed back and forth, driving Jade into mindlessness. He heard her incoherent entreaties, understanding the essence of her plea if not the words. He finally settled on one aching breast, his hand encompassing the fullness of the other as his lips and teeth marauded relentlessly across and around her engorged nipple.

Jade ran her fingers down through the dense hair that covered his chest. Just as he slid his fingers across her abdomen, she trailed her fingertips in a corresponding manner. Gathering her courage, she reached for him and closed her hand around him. She moaned, as much in response to the hard smooth heat of him as to his disposal of the single barrier covering her body.

They explored together, simultaneously setting off flaring little bursts of fire within each other. Jade arched off the bed when Reed cupped the heat and residual wetness of her body with his hand. She cried out again and again—gasping little cries of pleasure that made her sound agonized and untamed—when he tested the receptivity of her body with his fingers and used his thumb on the nub of sensitivity hidden beneath a cluster of dark curls.

She responded instinctively, caressing his arousal as he stroked the most delicate part of her. He stoked her inner fire with focused intent, his fingers firm but gentle, his lips and teeth still at her nipples. He drew the spiraling tension in her tighter and tighter until she thought she would detonate from the force of the storm raging within.

Covered in sweat and barely able to breathe, Reed caught her hand and fell back across the bed as the air jerked in and out of his lungs. She followed him and wound up half sprawled across his chest, her fingers on an intentional route back down toward his hips.

He couldn't speak, so he simply tried to catch his breath while he struggled for control. He finally drew her the rest of the way atop him, diverting her restless hands in the process. He positioned her astride him, just as he had before, but this time there were no barriers, nothing that could separate them.

Jade leaned forward, shifted her hips and then settled slowly back down, shocking him with the unexpected swiftness and ease of her acquisition. "I want you," she whispered as she leaned forward and kissed his chin.

"You've got me, sweet lady, and all that I am."

He held her shoulders so that she remained in a half crouch above him. He kissed her, slowly, with exquisite tenderness and consummate skill. When he released her lips and she was panting breathlessly, he asked, "Now that you have me, what are you going to do with me?"

She looked startled for a moment, but then she began to move. She felt awkward at first, but the feeling soon disappeared. Reed reclaimed her mouth and imitated with his tongue what another part of his anatomy was doing. Jade clenched her fingers, unaware of the biting fierceness of her grip on his shoulders as she picked up her pace. She felt glorious, like a bird soaring high into the sky.

Reed's head fell back. He gritted his teeth and guided Jade's hips, his own rising up to meet and mate fully with her. His breathing, already harsh, grew even more ragged.

Air whooshed in and out of her. Perspiration trailed down her neck and across her chest to mingle with the sweat that beaded his powerful torso. She threw her head back, her eyes falling closed, her neck arching, her teeth dragging repeatedly at her lower lip. Reed answered every dip and sway of her hips with a thrusting surge of hard flesh.

She moaned and held on tighter, trusting instinct and Reed more than anything else. Their passion exploded. Thought became impossible, control was flagrantly abandoned.

Their bodies met, parted almost completely, and then plunged together with frenzied rhythm in a series of frantic movements. Jade felt the coil of tension curling inside her snap suddenly. Reed felt the quickening within her, that exquisite milking sensation brought on by the contractions that began with gentle tremors and then built to a staggering force.

She triggered his body without any awareness of her own power. Her contractions quickly intensified. He responded, his own body arching up off the bed and exploding within her. Even as he reached the precipice, cried out her name and then tumbled forward into an abyss filled with sensation and warmth, he felt Jade come apart in his arms under the staggering impact of her own release.

He held her steady as she continued to push against him. Fascinated, he watched the almost blissful look that settled across her face, the unsteady rise and fall of her perspiration-damp breasts, and the tears of uncertain origin that began to slide down her cheeks.

He held her when she would have collapsed, fighting off the malaise invading his own limbs as he gently lowered her into a sexy sprawl across his chest. Her insides continued to quiver, and he could feel even the subtlest of the tiny quakes that sporadically shook her.

Jade couldn't stop her tears—tears of utter joy at the heartbreaking beauty of what she'd just shared with Reed. Nothing had prepared her for the experience or for the flood of emotion now submerging her soul.

She didn't move. She couldn't have, even if she'd wanted to. She didn't even feel inclined to speak. Too content and too fulfilled, she was reluctant to separate herself from Reed's body or his embrace.

She felt safe. She felt secure. And she felt cared for, perhaps for the first time since the deaths of her mother and father. Closing her eyes, she drifted off, clasped gently against Reed's chest.

His weary mind and troubled thoughts focused completely on the woman in his arms, he sighed her name as fatigue claimed him.

Seven

———

Darkness cloaked the California coastline. Although it was nearly midnight, Jade and Reed lingered at the dining-room table long after finishing their late meal. They chatted on topics as diverse as the space shuttle, the economy in Latin America, and the moral implications of any society preoccupied with the acquisition of *things*.

After a lull in the conversation, Jade verbalized a subject that still intrigued her. Without stopping to think, she simply remarked, "I can't imagine why your ex-wife was unfaithful to you. Did you ever figure out the cause?"

Reed smiled at her even as he shook his head. She never ceased to amaze him. Even more amazing to him was the fact that Pam's infidelity no longer seemed important. Still, he leaned back in his chair and considered how to respond.

The failure of his first marriage had hurt him, of course, but new challenges, personal maturation and the passage of time had helped him regain his perspective. It was only when he was under pressure or if he felt emotionally vulnerable that he remembered the anguish of that failed relationship.

He recalled the night he'd walked into his quarters in base housing and discovered his beautiful young wife in bed with another man. There had been rumors for months concerning her infidelity, and sly looks from men who, he later discovered, had sampled her charms; but he'd stubbornly ignored the innuendos, the nagging sensation that all wasn't right on the home front. Youthful pride and a fragile ego, he eventually realized, had kept him from wanting to know the truth.

As he put the pieces of his life back together after their divorce, he also realized that he hadn't wanted to believe her capable of betrayal. He hadn't wanted to accept that she couldn't be like the loyal wives of his friends, or that she didn't possess the courage and inner strength to stand by him or to accept the sometimes impossible demands of his military career.

Jade regretted her impulsive comment when she saw the play of emotions on Reed's face. Still, she felt torn. She wanted to understand why Reed's marriage had failed. She needed to know why he'd hurled the information at her like a deadly weapon during an earlier conversation at the center. She also wondered if he considered all women unworthy of his trust as a result of that negative experience.

"I'm sorry, Reed. I guess I didn't think about how rude I might sound. I've always been very good at opening my mouth and inserting both feet. It was thoughtless of me to pry and probe into your past."

When he didn't say anything, she shifted uneasily in her chair, silently hating her clumsiness. One of these years she hoped she would feel more confident as a woman, but for now she felt as though she'd fallen into an endless learning curve where a man like Reed was concerned.

"It's just that after tonight, well, I think she must have been a little crazy." She flushed when she noticed his lazy grin.

"Don't worry about it," he told her. "It happened a long time ago, when I was in the Marine Corps. We were both young—too young to be married and far too young to understand the kind of commitment involved. I was constantly deployed out of the country because of the work I did then. She couldn't handle being alone, so she found a way to fill the empty hours and an empty bed. It took me a long time to forgive her, but I think I finally have."

"But why—"

"It's not important." He stood abruptly. Pam represented the past. Jade symbolized the present. He didn't want anyone or anything to get in the way of their time together. "Let's take that walk."

Surprised by his behavior, she followed his progress around the table. Clad in a pair of running shorts, he was marvelous to look at with his tanned muscular torso, tight, flat stomach and strong thighs exposed to her view.

"Now?" she asked, faltering somewhat thanks to her fascination with his anatomy. "I'm not exactly dressed for a hike."

He reached for her, his eyes glowing at the thought of her naked body concealed beneath one of his shirts. He drew her to her feet and led her across the spacious living area and out onto the deck that faced the beach. "Why not now? You got a hot date, lady?"

She grinned up at him. "Yeah," she teased.

He gave her a dark look and then leaned down to plant a quick, hard kiss on her lips. "Think again, lady."

"A hot date with you," she hastily assured him as her grin grew even wider and she wagged her eyebrows at him. "Only with you."

He responded easily to her playfulness. "You're impossible."

"That's your opinion. Most people think I'm quite—*ooomph!*"

He'd stopped suddenly and swung her up and over his shoulder as though she weighed no more than a handful of feathers, then made his way down a short flight of steps. Understandably, Jade lost her train of thought.

The moon provided a limited source of light. Most of the homes and condominiums that lined the beach were dark, their residents already asleep.

Reed felt a lazy kind of contentment encompass him. He appreciated the peace and privacy of the deserted beachfront, as well as the woman beating playfully on his backside. He finally relented, responded to her muffled protests and helped her get her footing in the sand.

Jade pulled a hank of hair out of her mouth, tugged Reed's shirt back down to her thighs and laughed delightedly. For the first time in her life, she felt absolutely carefree.

"You're such a caveman, Townsend."

He felt a twinge of uneasiness at her remark, but he ruthlessly banished it. He wouldn't ever be anyone but who he was—a rough-edged and ambitious man of action. He knew he wasn't sophisticated, and his values were old-fashioned.

"You love it, lady, so don't complain."

She did, she realized. She loved everything about him. She loved *him*, but it was far too soon to express her emotions, and she couldn't think of a safe way to reveal the truth, anyway. If Reed knew the depth of her feelings for him, then he would have incredible power over her. That final realization silenced her.

Sifting through her jumbled thoughts, she tried to come up with a clever rejoinder to his last comment, but despite

er mental ransacking, she couldn't. They quietly wandered across the beach and down to the water's edge.

The surf lapped and gurgled at their feet as they paused
here, hand in hand. Several minutes of companionable si-
ence followed while they scuffed their way through the sand
and around a large tide pool near the north edge of the
beach. They headed toward the cliffs that joined Del Mar to
the neighboring Solana Beach. The jutting outcropping of
rock supported several condos and private homes and cast
a protective shadow across the beach below.

Reed sensed that Jade's prolonged silence was a cover for
a thousand and one questions. She was a chatty little thing,
a fact he'd discovered during and after dinner. And she was
as bright as a newly polished diamond.

Because she was well-read and well educated, he knew he
shouldn't have been surprised that she had deep feelings and
well-thought-out opinions on a world of subjects. It made
his limited schooling seem that much more inadequate, so
he tried not to dwell on their differences.

He also tried to ignore the voice in his head that urged him
to tell her the truth about his dual role in her life. Realisti-
cally, it was already too late. He knew that as well as he
knew his own name. He should have told her before they'd
made love. He hadn't, fool that he was. He had no choice
now. He had to do it soon.

"You're about to explode," he commented after Jade
sighed heavily for the third time. "So why don't you spit out
whatever it is that's got you tied up in knots?"

Reed assumed that the center was on her mind. It was the
only subject they hadn't touched on all evening. And it was
the one thing they needed to talk about.

She darted a glance in his direction. "I was just thinking
that even though I was involved with Mark for almost a
year, we never really made love. We had very mechanical sex

that left me feeling inadequate as a partner and edgy for reasons I didn't understand then. Now, though, I do." She shrugged awkwardly. "Tonight surprised me, that's all."

He paused to study her in the soft glow of the moonlight. Her frankness was like the shock of a bullet fired point-blank at his heart. He wondered if she realized how unusual she was.

"What surprised you about it?" he asked quietly.

She looked up at him, her vulnerability obvious in the big eyes that dominated the pale oval of her face. "That you could make me feel so much. That I could burn up inside and then survive the blaze. And that I could be so satisfied that I fell asleep sprawled across you for almost an hour. I was right, you know. You're quite the lover—very skilled and too talented to be believed."

"It's never been that way for me, either. I won't deny that I've had other women, Jade, but it's been almost two years since I was involved with anyone. With you, though, it's different."

"Different?" she echoed.

He heard the uneasiness in her voice. "Different as in good. Different as in exciting. Different as in fulfilling and earth-shattering, all at the same time. Look, I'm not clever with words, but what happened tonight went beyond the physical for me, Jade."

She reached out, her fingertips hesitant as she ran them up and down his arm. "You made me feel special."

"You *are* special."

Jade didn't know what to say. No one had ever told her that she was special before, and she wanted desperately to believe that Reed was sincere. Feeling uncertain, she started to turn away. He stopped her by catching her hand.

"What's wrong?"

She shook her head, glad that he couldn't see the flush of heat consuming her entire body.

"Talk to me, Jade."

"I want you again," she whispered.

He groaned and reeled her in against his body. He felt his pulse jump forward into a gallop. "You're embarrassed."

She glared up at him before she buried her face in the tawny fur that covered his broad chest.

The wash of her warm breath and the feel of her soft cheek made his nerves tingle. When she tucked her fingers beneath the stretchy waistband of his running shorts and held on to his narrow waist, he shuddered.

"I guess you only *think* you want me."

"I *know* I want you, Reed Townsend."

"That's a relief," he deadpanned. "I was afraid you were just toying with my affections."

Startled, she looked up at him. She quickly realized that he was teasing, but she didn't get a chance to say anything, because Reed tugged her several yards down the beach to the shelter of a cluster of boulders at the base of the cliff.

Despite the fact that local teenagers frequently used the area at night as a quasi-lovers' lane during the summer months, the beach was empty. The lifeguard towers, occupied year-round during the day because of the California climate, stood like silent sentries at precise intervals up and down the beach. Reed didn't even notice the usual after dark bonfires he was accustomed to seeing on sultry summer nights.

He leaned against a smooth hunk of rock and then tugged Jade back against his chest. The salty air caressed their faces and skimpily clad bodies. They watched the night-lights of an airplane as it flew at low altitude on a route parallel to the coast. The stars winked at them periodically, and the moon continued to glow softly in the black velvet sky.

Reed's conscience did a double-time march through his head, reminding him that an honorable man didn't take advantage of a woman's trust. "I need to talk to you about the center," he began.

"Why?"

He cleared his throat and tightened his arms around her midriff. His muscles clenched and unclenched with the movement. "There's something I have to—"

She suddenly twisted in his arms and looked up at him. Her shirt twisted, too. He felt the erotic swipe of her hip against his groin as she turned, and then the warm and soft tangle of dark silk at the top of her bare thighs as she settled between his parted legs. His body, already painfully aware of hers, lurched to life.

Jade smiled—that sweet feminine smile that belongs to a woman who is just discovering her own sexual power. "No shoptalk tonight. This is all too perfect to ruin with a heavy dose of reality. Reality, whatever its form, is definitely not welcome here. We can always discuss business tomorrow, but no sooner, please—"

"Jade, we should talk," Reed insisted. He stopped insisting when she trailed her fingertips down his chest to his tense flat stomach.

"It's still so hot out," she murmured.

He unconsciously held his breath.

"*You're* so hot," she marveled in a throaty voice as she worked his running shorts free of his hips and slid them down his sturdy thighs.

She lightly scraped her fingernails back and forth across his lower abdomen. She felt his response nudging against her, searching for a home between her legs. She took him into her hands and gently stroked his hard flesh.

Reed felt his body surge in response. He drew in a sharp breath and grasped the lapels of Jade's shirt. He abruptly yanked the fabric apart. Buttons popped and scattered in several different directions. He lowered his head and took her mouth while his hands charted a direct course to her swollen taut-nippled breasts.

His last coherent thought was profound gratefulness that Jade had inadvertently used herself as an obstacle and delayed his revelation of his identity as her anonymous caller. He would tell her later, he decided. Perhaps on the telephone since she obviously trusted him in his role as confidant and potential benefactor.

She couldn't stop herself from touching him and wanting him, nor would she deny herself the pleasure of the experience. She felt greedy after so many years of emotional and physical starvation.

Tearing her mouth from his, she filled her lungs with much-needed air. And she said again the words that she'd said before, this time in a voice filled with hushed wonder, "You're so hot, Reed. Your skin's almost on fire. I want your fire inside me."

"I'll make you hot, sweet lady," he promised in a voice so rough that chill bumps rose on Jade's skin. "I'll make you so hot you'll be screaming for me."

She groaned and raised her arms to circle his neck. "I feel so much when we make love."

He lifted her so that her breasts were level with his mouth. Before capturing a distended nipple, he urged, "Don't hold back, Jade. Let yourself feel everything. Yell if you need to, but don't hold anything back."

I love you, she realized as she spoke freely in the privacy of her heart. *I love you so much.*

She bit her lip against the words, but they continued to echo in her head and tap-dance around her heart like a choreographed number with each sucking pull of his mouth on her nipples. She cupped his face with her hands and wrapped her slender legs around him. Pressing forward, she felt the throbbing ache deep inside her intensify.

Reed nearly dropped her when he felt the rhythmic invitation of her lower body. He fell to his knees in the sand and brought them loin to loin. His entry was slow and seductive, just like the way he plunged his tongue past her lips and teeth and ravaged the soft interior of her mouth.

Jade held tightly to him, her hips surging forward, her flesh burning and her mouth duplicating the action of her body.

Reed slid erotically in and out of her, making her cry out with each driving thrust and every pulsing withdrawal. Finally he buried himself within her and held her still, struggling to hold back, struggling to sustain the tension coiled around their bodies.

He felt her inner muscles tense and throb, quake and clench in anticipation of what was to come. The sensation prompted a strangled groan and almost set him off. He struggled again and finally managed to drag his mouth from hers and draw in enough air to calm himself somewhat.

"Reed, you're driving me out of my mind!"

He laughed with a sound that was raspy, out of control. "No quickies with you, Jade. I want this to last."

"You're torturing me," she protested as she undulated against him and reclaimed his mouth.

"I love it when you're aggressive," he whispered against her lips as he fell victim to the rhythm of her hips and the trembling little muscles in the interior of her body.

"Reed, now, please!" she gasped.

The sweet plea of the woman and the demanding seduction of her femininity pushed him over the edge. He answered her plea, he met her demand, and he pushed her far beyond the edge.

She cried out.

He inhaled the sound into his own mouth.

She dug her fingernails into his shoulders.

He didn't even feel the pain.

She trembled just before her contractions gained strength and took complete control of her.

He instantly felt the change. Her pleasure swept over him like a tidal wave, consuming him, devastating him, draining him and then leveling him as it brought about his own. The power of the experience forced him back onto his haunches as he clutched her to his heaving chest.

A shaft of moonlight fell across their joined bodies. Sensually entwined, they looked remarkably like a piece of living sculpture.

Reed watched Jade through narrowed eyes, his expression pained with pleasure, his breathing choppy. He saw the exposed column of her throat, the convulsive swallowing, her parted lips, the air entering and exiting her in panting gasps, her closed eyes, the thick fringe of her eyelashes like half-moons of mink on her delicate cheekbones, her forehead, dotted with perspiration that gathered her bangs in irregular clumps.

He knew at that moment that he'd been granted a temporary restraining order on the inevitable.

They scrambled out of bed when Reed's alarm sounded early the next morning. Jade spent as much time in the shower slapping at Reed's hands as she did soaping and rinsing her body. He drove her to her apartment and made instant coffee while she hurriedly changed into clean clothes. As he drank the strong brew, Reed inspected her tiny refuge from the world.

There was little to set the apartment apart from thousands of others like it. The living/dining/kitchen area constituted one room and ninety percent of Jade's "home." It finally occurred to him that the couch doubled as a fold-out bed, because other than the bathroom and a small closet, there weren't any other rooms in the place.

The studio apartment was spotless, the limited furniture well-worn but clean, and the walls bare save for a faded reproduction he assumed someone had once considered acceptable apartment "art." What struck him as oddly discordant was the impersonal quality of her environment. That such a unique woman hadn't left her mark on her habitat troubled him and reminded him, as if he even needed reminding, that the sole focus of her life was elsewhere.

A twisted grapevine wreath decorated with dried wildflowers hung on the wall above the sink. Reed's mood grew somewhat melancholy at this glimpse of Jade's rather barren existence, and he had to force himself to smile at her when she emerged from the bathroom.

He handed her a mug of coffee after giving her a swift, hard hug. "All set?"

She nodded, preoccupied as she inventoried the contents of her purse, added some tissue and a lipstick and then collected a stack of folders from the coffee table in front of the couch.

"Bring your coffee with you, why don't you?"

She smiled up at him. "Good idea."

They stepped outside. Reed checked the door to make sure it was locked while Jade looked on, a peaceful expression on her face as she watched him. He turned, drew her protectively against the hard lines of his body and then escorted her back to his truck.

Reed joined the masses on the freeway, situated his vehicle in the middle lane of the slow-moving traffic and settled back for what would likely be a fifteen- or twenty-minute drive to the center.

He glanced at Jade. "You're a talkative little thing in the morning, aren't you?"

She made a sound, something between a groan and a sigh, and took another sip of coffee.

He reached out, slipped his hand under her skirt and stroked her thigh. Jade grinned into her mug, scooted to the left on the leather seat and tucked her slender hand between his thighs. Reed made a strangled sound.

He stepped on the brake and narrowly avoided attaching his truck to the rear fender of the Mercedes creeping along in front of him. "Woman, you're gonna be the death of me!"

She smiled angelically at him. "That'll teach you to try and do two things at once."

He slipped his hand higher. He felt her thigh muscles tense and then quiver. He felt her heat. And he felt his own body surge to life with swiftly kindled need.

Jade couldn't ignore his touch or the effect it had on her pulse. "Reed, you're going to have an accident!"

He gripped the steering wheel with his other hand and managed to speak, even as he stroked her inner thigh and despite the sizzle in his blood. "That's okay. I could use a little excitement in my life."

She shook her head, amazed by the desire he could evoke with a single touch or a heated glance. Moving back to her side of the bench seat, she couldn't recall a time when she'd been happier.

Jade finished her coffee as they left the freeway and merged onto the equally crowded streets at the edge of downtown San Diego. Content, she didn't say anything until Reed stopped at a red light a few blocks from the center.

"Would you pull over to the curb across the street?"

He did as she asked as soon as the light turned green and he could move out of the flow of traffic. "What's wrong?

Are you sick?'' he asked as she gathered up her purse and folders and reached for the door handle.

"Of course not." She slid out of the truck, slammed the door and peered through the open window. "I'm fine, really."

"Then what in sweet hell are you doing?" he demanded.

"I'm walking the rest of the way."

Reed just stared at her as though she'd lost her mind.

"I refuse to put on a show for your construction crew, Reed Townsend. I'll see you at the center."

The word he bellowed couldn't have been repeated except perhaps in hell or at a gathering of marines. Jade ignored Reed's outburst and started walking, although she did flinch when he left a streak of rubber on the pavement.

Pausing at the newsstand at the next corner, she purchased the morning paper. She didn't have much time to think about Reed's touchy behavior once she walked into the center a few minutes later. He was nowhere in sight, but his construction crew—two dozen men and three women, in hard hats—was well into the workday despite the early hour.

The phone calls, a veritable glut of them, started shortly after eight and continued into the afternoon.

Two TV network affiliates, a cable talk show, four radio stations, a north country magazine, one high school journalism teacher, the Rotary Club, several religious organizations and a collection of men's and women's clubs looking for speakers called to express interest in the Activity Center.

Jade barely had time to catch her breath before a second round of calls came in, this time primarily from private parties interested in making modest donations to the Activity Center's account at the local bank.

She managed to read Mick Everett's full page feature in the *Union* while she had a quick lunch at a small coffee shop near the center. After gently smoothing the creases from the paper with trembling hands, she blotted her tears with a tissue she found in her purse once she'd finished reading.

The article was beyond her wildest dreams, and she now understood why so many people had called her.

Mick Everett had carefully avoided being melodramatic. Instead, the newspaperman had used the facts and presented the center, its moral and practical value to the community, and its director, in a realistic light. In doing so, he'd still managed to evoke positive emotion and an outpouring of compassion for the children of homeless families.

A truck from a local toy manufacturer arrived just as Jade returned from lunch. It was filled with games and toys for children of all ages. Reed's workers helped unload and store the unexpected bounty in a vacant storeroom.

Meanwhile, Reed, cut to the quick by Jade's attitude, had driven to his corporate offices in Mission Valley, where he'd managed to alienate half of his senior level management staff during the course of the morning.

Only his sister, who worked as his receptionist, seemed unfazed. Her remark, "Must be a new woman in your life. It's about time, big brother," drew a hostile scowl and a few unrepeatable words.

She laughed outright and threatened, "Be nice, or I'll call mom and tell her you're in a snit about something. You know she always bakes you those inedible brownies of hers when she thinks you're upset."

Reed didn't want to deal with his mother, so he shut his mouth and stalked back into his office. He spent the morning and his lunch hour cooling off. He then tacked on another few hours to the process in order to accept the merit of Jade's behavior. She was right. And he knew it, even if he hated it.

He could understand her aversion to being a topic of speculative conversation among his men, but he still hurt a little inside. It took him a while before he accepted the fact that he was actually afraid that she was ashamed of him and of what they'd shared.

He kept trying to direct his mind back to business, but he continued to think about Jade, her sensuality, her explosive passion, and how much he wanted her, even now. He felt as though his body was punishing him for being such a jerk. He worked vigorously to eliminate the sense of rejection he also felt, but he didn't ever completely shake the feeling.

Flushed with excitement, Jade virtually glowed when Reed walked into her office at the center late that afternoon. A hectic interview-and-speech schedule rested at her elbow as she finished applying postage to the press kits stacked in front of her.

How could she look so happy? Reed wondered sourly. His good sense took a vacation. "Would you like to explain this morning?"

She gave him a blank look. "Which part of the morning?" she asked. She'd been on the phone nearly all day. Maybe he had tried to call.

He slammed the door shut. The ceiling produced a light snowfall of plaster, but neither of them paid much attention to what was becoming a routine event.

Jade stared at him, completely baffled by his behavior.

Reed stood in the center of the room, a scowl on his face, his body tense and ready for battle. "I'm talking about your hike to work, Ms. Howell. Are you ashamed that we slept together?" he demanded.

Shocked and angry, Jade jumped to her feet, although she remained behind her desk. She didn't see the vulnerability in Reed's expression as his words echoed in her ears. "Of all the witless, shortsighted, egotistical, *male* things to say, that takes the cake."

Reed looked stricken. Jade finally noticed how strained he seemed. She forced herself to take a deep breath and calm down. Yelling never had, and very likely never would, accomplish anything productive, she reminded herself. Besides, she wanted him to be happy for her.

"Reed, your men adore you. They watch everything you do. Why, some of the younger guys even imitate the way you walk and the way you dress. And they don't miss a move you make, especially when we're together. Haven't you ever noticed how attentive they are?"

"Jade..."

She waved him to silence. "Don't say anything yet. Just listen, please. I can't and won't become a topic for gossip. My status as director of the center is too important, and I can't have anyone questioning my morals or my values. I work with children, and that makes me particularly vulnerable to questions about my conduct. I've never had to worry about this kind of thing before, but now I do. Outside funding is crucial to the center. Do you think people will donate money to a cause that's run by a woman who sleeps around?"

"You don't sleep around! And we've only spent one night together. You've hardly given anyone a reason to accuse you of moral turpitude."

She moved around her desk. "And I'm not going to start now, because I don't plan to ruin everything I've spent the past eighteen months building. I'm sorry if you don't understand, but I'm not going to change my mind."

"Are you telling me we're finished before we've even started?"

"Of course not!" she exclaimed, horrified that he would even think or suggest such a thing. "I'm not saying anything of the kind. I'm simply trying to tell you that being somewhat circumspect about our behavior is an excellent idea."

"I'm trying to understand," he insisted, his fists pressed tightly to his thighs. *Circumspect,* he thought disgustedly. *Sneaking around* was what she really meant.

Jade grabbed her makeshift calendar and shoved it at him. He had no choice but to accept it.

"Look at that. Just look at what's happened because of the full page feature about the center in the morning paper."

He'd seen the newspaper, of course, and then he'd wadded it up and thrown it into the trash can. Granted, he knew he was being childish, but he hadn't been thinking too clearly at the time. As soon as he'd read the article, he realized it would produce results, and those results would translate into less time with Jade.

Excited, Jade waited for his reaction as long as she could, but he just stared at the schedule she'd made. "Isn't it fabulous? Do you realize how many people I'm going to be able to reach? Hundreds, maybe even thousands. I can tell them about the kids and the center," she enthused. "One reporter even called me the crusader for the disadvantaged."

He didn't like the sound of that at all. The idea of her becoming some public symbol bothered him. He could feel her slipping away from him already. "Don't let your ego get out of control, Jade. The downside of that kind of a trip can be a real disaster."

"I don't care what they call me," she answered dismissively. "They can call me Little Bo-peep if they want to, just as long as they give me a shot at the public. Reed, why do you have such a negative attitude all of a sudden? You must realize how much all this means to me, and you've seen how hard I've worked. If you care about me at all, then you'll be happy for me."

He didn't say anything for a moment. He considered the sincerity of her motives and her single-minded dedication to homeless children. He also realized how selfishly he was reacting.

"You're right. My attitude stinks, but what you did this morning bothered the hell out of me."

Jade's expression softened. She slipped into his arms and sighed with relief when he hugged her to him.

"How could you possibly think that I'd be ashamed of you or what we've shared? Last night was incredible, and I loved every minute of it." She eased back so that she could see his face. "I'd never purposely hurt you."

He tugged her back into his arms and simply held her. And he let her talk him out of his bad mood. When she stopped speaking and snuggled intimately between his parted thighs, he asked, "How about a repeat performance of last night?"

"How about a quiet dinner?" she countered before she found the courage to admit in a muffled whisper, "I'm a little tender right now."

He stepped back and raised her face with his fingertips, not sure if he'd heard her correctly.

Jade flushed and ducked her head. "It's been a long time for me, you know."

He roared with laughter—not at her discomfort but at her marvelous candor. His amusement faded quickly, though, and he looked down at her with heart-stopping tenderness. "Sweet lady, you're one surprise after another. I'm glad you said something, though, because it would kill me if I hurt you."

She grinned and stage-whispered, "We'll make up for my...ah...temporary incapacitation soon. I promise."

He made a great show of considering her suggestion. "You college girls are so clever and you have such a way with words, but I think you should just tell people you've been horseback riding for the past week if anyone notices that you're walking funny."

"I'm not walking funny!" She looked uncertain for a moment and then demanded, "Am I?"

He laughed even harder at that. Jade grinned, a wicked little grin that made her eyes dance and promised tormenting retribution before she was finished with him. He hugged her to him with startling fierceness, his desire for her and his need of her growing at an alarming pace.

Reed suddenly realized that her earthy attitude and contrary nature were in sharp contrast to the professional decorum required of her and the responsibilities that weighed so heavily on her slender shoulders. He promised himself that he would stop acting like a fool, maintain a supportive attitude even if it drove him crazy, and make the most of whatever time they could manage together.

Eight

Reed Townsend loathed feeling helpless. Still, he experienced the impotent fury of a man forced, by his own actions, to walk a tightrope between two identities.

Having waited two full weeks, he was now ready to make his third anonymous call to Jade. He worried constantly about the long hours she put in and used that worry to justify delaying the inevitable. But the truth needed telling. His conscience and his sense of honor offered him no other alternative.

Eighteen-hour workdays had become the norm for Jade, thanks to the media's interest in the Activity Center. It seemed that everyone wanted a piece of this articulate, sincere and dedicated woman—*his* woman, he amended mentally, if only for the time being.

Seated in a lounge chair on the deck of his house, Reed broodingly nursed the inch or so of bourbon he'd splashed into the bottom of a glass. He watched the sun slowly sink to the edge of the horizon, his thoughts focused on the woman who had shared his bed each night for the past fourteen days. He was almost grateful that Jade was at the center, working on a speech she was scheduled to deliver the following morning to a local community group known for its successful fund-raising.

She labored like a mini-Trojan, repeatedly justifying the impossible schedule she'd designed for herself with the comment, "Timing is everything. People are interested now, but they might not be in a month or two. All this work will pay off in the long run."

She was working, all right, he thought in total frustration. She was working herself right into the ground.

He'd lost track of the times he'd carried her upstairs to bed, undressed her, tucked her slender body against his own and held her for the four or five hours of sleep she allowed herself each night. She stubbornly refused to ease up. He'd finally stopped harping on the subject, but only after vowing to himself that he would be there for her whenever she needed him, and for as long as she would allow herself to need him.

Reed placed his drink on the deck railing, tugged a Paisley bandanna from his hip pocket and reached for the phone. He punched out the numbers he knew by heart and waited for the voice of the woman who had changed the definition of his life.

She answered almost immediately. "Activity Center."

Reed heard the fatigue layered subtly beneath the upbeat tone of her voice. "It appears that you've been burning the candle at both ends, Jade. You're a difficult lady to reach these days."

She laughed, the sound so seductive to Reed's ears. He tightened his grip on the receiver and reminded himself of the role he was now playing and the truth that had to be told.

Jade leaned back in her chair and smiled. "I'm so glad you've called."

He felt a primitive surge of satisfaction. His decision not to contact her by phone as Reed, while selfishly motivated, had been the right thing to do, he realized.

"How've you been?" she asked.

"Not quite as busy as you, I suspect."

"I wondered when you'd call next."

"Missed me, have you?" he asked, forcing a light, teasing note into his question.

She paused briefly, aware that she *had* missed him. "As a matter of fact, I have."

"I'm surprised," Reed admitted, filled with a mix of pleasure and dismay. That Jade missed someone other than him didn't do a lot for his confidence, or his conscience.

"Why?"

"I've been following your activities. The press appears to have adopted you. I would imagine you're having trouble finding enough time for a few hours of sleep each night. Idle thought doesn't exactly fit into your current schedule."

"Isn't it wonderful? Everyone seems interested in the center these days," she enthused. "By the way, you're hardly a topic for idle thought."

He didn't know quite how to respond to that last remark, so he pursued the course of his own thoughts. "I hope you aren't pushing yourself too hard."

She groaned. What was it with the male population? They worried like little old ladies. "Now you sound like a friend of mine."

"A *concerned* friend?"

She smiled at the wry note in his voice. "A man I know."

"The man we talked about last time?"

"That's right."

"So you've changed your mind about going it alone?"

"In a way," she agreed. "To be perfectly honest, I'm not really certain where we're headed."

"Then I won't intrude on your privacy and ask what you want in your relationship with him."

"I wouldn't mind if you asked," she conceded, her voice subdued. "I just don't have an answer."

Reed exhaled a gust of air. His heart felt like a dead weight in his chest, and his emotions seemed in total disarray. He'd reminded himself often enough that he shouldn't plan more than one day at a time with Jade. Her comment now served to reinforce that reminder.

"Is something wrong?" Jade asked after several quiet moments.

"Nothing you need to worry about."

"If you'd like to talk about something that's bothering you, I'm more than willing to listen."

"Why don't we stick to the center for the time being?"

"Whatever you want," she agreed. He didn't sound like himself, and she wondered why. But she respected him too much to push him.

"You do realize that all this interest in the Activity Center might be short-lived, don't you?"

"Oh, of course. That's the reason I'm trying to do as much as possible right now."

Reed moved on to the next obvious question. "Are the donations from the public what you'd hoped for?"

She hesitated. She knew she had to voice the issue that preyed so heavily on her mind, so she answered carefully, "As far as the funds needed for our operating capital, yes."

"I get the impression that something isn't quite right, Jade."

Instinct urged her to share the secret she'd kept from everyone, even Reed. "You've hit the nail on the head, as usual."

"Tell me about it."

"I've got a major problem," she answered bluntly.

Alarmed, Reed straightened in his chair. If she had a major problem, as she put it, why in the hell didn't he know about it? "Sounds serious."

She sighed. "It is."

"I think you'd better tell me about it, then."

"One of the reasons I've been happy about your calls is because I believe your interest in the Activity Center is sincere. Another reason is that I trust you, despite the fact that we've never actually met." She paused, carefully weighing her words before she continued. "Last time we talked, I explained some of our financial needs."

"Monthly overhead for the center once the renovation work is completed, plus funding for specialized counseling," he clarified.

Jade took a steadying breath and forged ahead. "That's right. What I didn't tell you is that I don't have enough money to make the final payment on the renovations."

Stunned, Reed grappled with the shock reeling through his mind. His plan to reveal his dual identity fell by the wayside. He didn't even think about the money she owed his company. He could only wonder why she hadn't trusted him with the truth of her situation? Why did she persist in doing battle with the world alone?

"How much?" he asked, amazed that he could even speak.

"Barring a minor miracle, I don't think I can pay the bill, even with the donation money that's coming in."

"How much, Jade?" he demanded, his voice terse as he struggled with his emotions. With so many jobs under way at Foothills Construction, he really didn't recall the exact amount.

"Thousands. I know I shouldn't have, but I was counting on the Lindley Foundation grant money. It's not as though I was kidding myself. The director all but assured me the center would receive the money, but then he changed his mind," she whispered. "I don't know what I'm going to do, especially since I have to come up with the money within the next three weeks."

"Have you explained your situation to Mr. Townsend?"

"Not yet."

"May I ask why not?"

"You can ask me anything," she hastily assured him.

"Tell me."

"Do you remember our conversation about me needing someone in my life? Well, I have someone now, but the man is Reed Townsend."

"He's a complication you hadn't counted on, isn't he?" Reed asked bitterly.

"Yes."

"Did you think about that before you slept with him?"

"No," she replied in a small voice. "I guess I didn't think at all." Belatedly she asked, "How did you know we'd slept together?"

"Would you be this worried if you hadn't?"

"I guess not."

Reed fell silent. He felt irrational, crazed, almost like an animal desperate for survival. "Did you sleep with him for the sake of the center, Jade?" he asked tensely.

"Why I slept with Reed Townsend isn't even the point!" she exclaimed. "You've got to be a lawyer. No one reminds me of a dentist's drill more than a lawyer."

He laughed, but the sound wasn't pleasant. It reminded Jade of fury-filled thunder.

"Then you aren't a lawyer."

"That's right, I'm not." He refused to be redirected by her question. "Why didn't you tell me about this situation before?"

"I was working up to it. Heavens! I was praying for a miracle, if you want the truth. I really hate asking for money, so I try to wait for the subject to come up naturally. Look, getting anyone to donate money to a worthy cause is like conducting courtship rituals."

At that moment, Reed considered her quite skilled in the seductive arts. He also considered himself a complete fool. "Are you asking me for money now?"

"I'm asking for help, if you can give it." She sighed heavily, aware that the harmony they'd shared was now gone. "I've made a commitment to Foothills Construction—a commitment I honestly believed I could meet. I also thought the Lindley Foundation would come through with the grant money, but they didn't."

"And now you're stuck somewhere between a rock and a hard place with only your pride for company?"

"That's about the size of things."

He ignored the morose sound of her voice. He didn't feel compassionate at the moment. He didn't feel anything except numbness.

"Why not tell Reed Townsend the truth?"

"I don't want him to think I'm using him."

"Aren't you?"

The tone of his voice stunned her. "You're angry."

"I'm not angry." He realized that he was speaking the truth. What he actually felt was best described as anguish, not anger. Part of him respected her determination to achieve her goals, while another part of him felt the keen bite of betrayal. "Do you care about him at all?"

Ever protective of her emotions, she cautiously admitted, "He's different from anyone I've ever known."

He's a fool! Reed thought to himself. "You'll have to tell him."

"Not if I solve the problem on my own."

"When you do tell him," Reed persisted, "he's apt to think you've used him."

"Believe me, that's already occurred to me," she said.

Reed couldn't take much more of their conversation. "If you'll tell me the exact amount of the final payment, I'll look into the matter."

"Seventeen thousand dollars."

"Should I assume that you're simply transferring funds from the center's account whenever a payment is due?"

"Yes."

"And you haven't received enough in donations?"

"Less than a third of what I owe."

"All right, Jade," he responded heavily.

"You're willing to help me pay part of the bill?"

"I said there's no need to worry. Foothills Construction doesn't concern you any longer."

Why didn't she feel relieved? Jade wondered. And why did she suddenly feel empty and lonely inside? "I don't know how to thank you."

"Then don't."

Startled by his coldness, she asked, "Why don't you want to be thanked? I don't understand."

"There's nothing to understand," he told her, the words coming out of his mouth like the sharp clicking of a thousand falling dominoes. "I told you at the outset that I was interested in the center. That hasn't changed."

But we have. She realized bleakly that he was disappointed in her. He was a man of courage and strength, and now he believed that she'd behaved like a manipulative coward. She didn't even know how to defend herself.

"Will you ever call me again?"

"I don't know, Jade," he admitted before he severed the phone connection.

Jade progressed through the next week on sheer nerve. She fought fatigue and the depression plaguing her over the loss of a unique friendship that had come to mean a great deal to her by burying herself in her work. Because she and Reed barely saw each other, except when she tumbled wearily into bed for a few hours of rest each night, his subdued manner and watchful expression didn't really register with her.

Grateful for his quiet strength, she sought comfort in his arms night after night. She also promised herself that she would reward his patience and understanding as soon as the chaos consuming her life became more manageable.

Reed moved through the same week in a state of nonverbal preoccupation that concerned friends and family alike. His refusal to share his feelings stymied everyone who cared about him, but he didn't seem to notice.

Caught up in the mixed emotions that haunted him day and night, he threw himself into his work with an almost frantic dedication. He hoped to sleep at night by pushing himself to the limit physically, but Jade's presence in his bed and the feel of her body burrowed into his when he held her kept him from vocalizing the betrayal he felt. He was torn between her needs and his own.

Damned by the emotional uncertainty he experienced as he tried to keep his dual roles in her life separate, he felt angry, frustrated and tense. He fully intended to admit his duplicity, but finding an appropriate moment now seemed impossible. Jade's exhaustion, her hectic schedule and his mounting anger over the secret she persisted in keeping from him, prevented any attempt at meaningful conversation.

Eight nights into the dilemma he'd helped create, he resorted to restless prowling up and down the stretch of beach behind his home.

Uneasiness crept into his consciousness with each step he took. He felt an almost acute sensitivity to Jade. He immediately abandoned his directionless hiking and made a beeline for his house.

As he raced up the stairs and across the back deck, Reed sensed at gut level that something was terribly wrong. Jade. He could feel her distress deep in his bones, as if she were calling out to him, beckoning him with her thoughts. He'd heard about telepathic communication, of course, but he'd never put much faith in it until now.

Grabbing the phone, he dialed the center, only to hear a busy signal. Mounting concern made him call the operator, who confirmed that the phone was off the hook. Reason told him that Jade might have taken such an action in order to work undisturbed, but his gut kept telling him something else altogether.

Reed abandoned logic and drew on his instincts. Seizing his car keys, he raced out of the house. He careened into the parking lot behind the center less than fifteen minutes later, scattering gravel as he skidded to a stop and jumped out of his truck. Having broken every speed law in the city, he fully expected a caravan of police cars to pull in behind him.

The night, however, remained eerily silent.

He quietly made his way across the dark lot, his face settling into grim lines when he discovered that the back doors to the center were unlocked. The voices he heard as he crept down the hallway to Jade's office, one quiet and fearful, the other high-pitched and threatening, increased the stealthiness of his approach.

One look at Jade sprawled on the dusty floor of her office with a man crouched over her, his face concealed beneath a ski mask and a knife clutched in his hand, robbed Reed of reason and control. He lunged toward the attacker with an enraged bellow and sent the man hurtling against the wall. Shoving Jade behind him, he turned on the man, murder in his eyes.

He unleashed his fury and meted out his own brand of justice in short order. The attacker soon cowered beneath Reed's punishing fists.

Meanwhile Jade dragged the phone into her lap after crawling to her desk. She shakily dialed 911 and gave directions in an oddly detached tone of voice that would have alarmed Reed if he'd heard it.

Reason gradually returned as he knelt over the man he'd beaten to the edge of senselessness. Bent over the incoherent man, Reed reared back and settled on his haunches when he felt Jade's hand on his shoulder.

His chest heaved as he sought control, while he absently opened and closed his bruised and bleeding hands to relieve the ache in them. Her voice finally penetrated the red haze that even now seemed reluctant to leave his mind.

Jade was frightened—but no longer of her attacker. She couldn't drag her eyes from the forbidding expression on Reed's face. His fury was etched harshly into the strong lines of his face as if cast in stone, with his inner rage still blazing in his dark eyes. She'd never seen him like this. She'd never seen anyone this angry, this capable of violence.

"I'm all right," she said slowly, forcing each word past a throat swollen and bruised by the cruel hands of her assailant. "You got here in time. He frightened me, but he didn't really hurt me."

Reed turned slowly and got to his feet, his body still tense, his mind unwilling to settle, his need to reassure himself about her well-being profoundly acute as he seized her and crushed her against his chest. Nothing else mattered.

She stood, shattered and shaking, in the shelter of his fierce embrace, but she managed to soothe him, as well as herself, by running her hands up and down his arms and across his shoulders as she clung to him. She fought the tormenting shock of the experience that she'd just had and held it at bay by focusing on Reed.

"I'm really okay, just a little shaken," she managed to tell him. "I gave him the money in the cashbox, but then he wanted to talk. He rambled for almost an hour, but nothing he said made any sense. He's probably on drugs. I . . . I didn't think he'd hurt me, but he . . . lost . . . control of . . ." She fell silent, her nerves shattered, her panic renewed.

Reed simply nodded as he stared down at her ashen face. Aware of his own violent loss of control, he couldn't help wondering if Jade feared him, too. His hands tightened on her when he felt the tremors shaking her slender body. She was beginning to react to what had just happened. A moment later they heard police and ambulance sirens.

While Jade gave a statement to the police, Reed let a paramedic tend his damaged knuckles. Then he watched silently as the paramedics checked the bruises at Jade's throat. He noted the advancing shock in her vacant, wide-eyed gaze and vowed that she would follow their advice about contacting her personal physician the next morning for a thorough examination.

He didn't let her out of his sight, but neither did he speak to her. For the first time in many years, he felt the disabling vulnerability inherent in loving. He didn't know when intense wanting had turned to loving, but he loved Jade. The realization staggered him, bewildered him and assured him that losing her would rob him of the very essence of his existence.

White-hot rage still filled him, as did his growing awareness that he'd lost the restraint that marks a civilized man.
He wore his shame like bulky armor, but he kept his fear of
losing her buried deep in his soul.

Jade concentrated on putting one foot in front of the
other when Reed escorted her to his truck and drove her to
the beach house. She knew she was on the edge. The slightest misstep would hurl her directly into hysterics.

She didn't question his silence after being extensively
quizzed by the arresting officers, although Reed's restraint
began to wear on her nerves as they drove into Del Mar. She
told herself that she was being foolish, that she needed time
to pull herself together; time to come to terms with what
could only be described as a life-threatening ordeal, before
she tried to make some sense of Reed's behavior.

They stood facing each other in the bedroom. She shivered uncontrollably when he reached for her.

He clenched his fists as his hands fell to his sides. Turning away, he experienced a flood of anguish at the sight of
the stark fear in her eyes. Fear of him, he realized bleakly.

"I need a shower."

She nodded and slowly sank to the edge of the bed. She
watched him disappear from sight, heard him turn on the
water, and then flinched when he slammed the glass shower
door. Shock kicked in again, threatening to consume her like
a ravaging illness. She stumbled toward the bathroom,
haphazardly shedding her clothes and leaving an untidy trail
along the way.

Naked, she stepped into the shower stall. Distracted by his
own remorse, Reed wasn't aware of her until she pressed
herself to his back and slid her arms around him.

He turned slowly in the circle of the arms tethered at his
waist. Looking down, he saw only the top of her head and
her shaking shoulders.

"Hold me, Reed," she whispered in a voice that shattered his uncertain emotions. "Please hold me."

She was like dynamite about to detonate. She clung to him, sobbing, hurting, shaking, until he feared for her sanity.

"Love me, Reed," she pleaded. "Love me, please. I don't want to be alone. I can't be alone any longer."

He wanted to be gentle, but he wasn't. He wanted to be tender and slow, but he wasn't capable of those things as she writhed against him. He sensed she wanted to crawl beneath his skin and bury herself inside him. He wanted to be in control, to put her first, but that wasn't possible, either.

Their loins slammed together as their hungry mouths and desperately searching hands satisfied earthy needs and explosive desire. The shower bench saved them from crashing to the floor in their haste, while the shower head pelted them almost erotically with pulsing jets of heated water.

She cried out repeatedly—irrational murmurs of need, demanding entreaties for more, and breathless words of pleasure—as he made pleasure explode inside her. He groaned as her hips quickened to a frantic pace, his own matching them and then surpassing hers in aggressiveness.

"Now, Reed. Now!"

He thrust up, high and hard, again and again. He felt her convulse and contract, even as he spewed his seed into her body. He felt her heated honey melting over him and basked in the sensations suffusing him as she continued to quake in his arms.

Slouched against the shower stall, with Jade still perched across his lap, he finally opened his eyes. Steamy mist enshrouded them and cocooned them from the world. Her eyes fluttered open—eyes still glazed with passion but eyes no longer filled with fear.

She slowly traced the side of his wet face with her finger-tips. Reed wasn't handsome, but he was compellingly masculine. He was also rough and tough and very much a product of what she suspected had been a hard life, although he seldom ever referred to his past. His financial success was apparent, but she sensed a loneliness in him, a kind of emptiness that all the money in the world couldn't alter or replenish.

"How did you know?" she finally found the strength to ask.

He exhaled heavily and leaned his head back against the wall. "I don't know. I just couldn't shake the feeling that something was wrong."

"Thank God for small favors," she whispered as she eased against his chest and tucked her face into the curving muscle and bone that flowed from his neck and shoulder.

His fingers dug into her hips. "I don't want you down there alone at night anymore."

"But..."

"No buts, Jade. The bastard was about to rape you and then slit your throat."

She shuddered and held on to him for dear life.

"No more risks, Jade." His voice trembled with emotion. "I wouldn't survive if something happened to you."

She nodded numbly as the shakes began to consume her once again. She shivered, shockingly chilled despite the heat of the shower and the warmth of Reed's sturdy body. Guiding her from the shower, he toweled her dry, wrapped her in a thick terry robe and carried her into the bedroom.

Throughout the night, she relived the assault in a series of nightmares, only to be restored to sanity by the passion she found in Reed's arms.

Nine

***

Reed glanced up from the cup of coffee he'd just poured for himself when Jade, dressed in burgundy silk slacks, a matching tunic top and high heels, walked into the kitchen. He watched her hesitate uncertainly in the center of the room. Sensing her uncharacteristic disquiet, he swiftly poured a second cup and carried it over to her.

She stared at the steaming black coffee, unable to meet his probing gaze. He muttered a harsh word when he noticed, once again, the dark fingerprint bruises circling her slender neck. She glanced up at him in surprise, but his intense look and the object of his focus explained the hostile sound quickly enough.

Jade lifted her free hand to her throat. Reed felt as if someone had just shoved a stake through his heart when he saw the vulnerability of the movement and the sudden welling of tears in her eyes. Tugging her hand from the evi-

dence of her assault, he silently led her out of the kitchen
and into the living room.

"I'd like five more minutes alone with that son of a—"

"Don't," she interrupted. "I want to forget he even exists."

Jade settled on the edge of one of the couches. Reed, clad
only in a pair of brief black running shorts, paced the room
like a hemmed-in product of some exotic jungle. "No more
late nights at the center," he burst out.

"But I—"

"No debates, Jade. You can't keep tempting fate this way.
You're gonna get yourself killed one of these nights."

"You're right," she conceded quietly.

"Of course I'm right!" he shouted.

She slid the half-empty coffee cup onto the low teak table in front of her with shaking hands. "Last night was awful. I'm not likely to forget what happened for a very long
time, if ever, so there's no need to yell at me, Reed."

His self-control slipped a notch. "There's every need to
yell, because that's about the only way I can get your attention. You're so damned buried in work that you're blind to
everything around you. Have you taken a good look in the
mirror lately?"

She straightened at that, her spine stiff with stung pride.
She knew she looked dented and bruised, not to mention
ragged around the edges. She had even resorted to wearing
sunglasses to cover the smudges of fatigue beneath her eyes.

"Who gave you the right to criticize me?"

"You did, when you crawled into my bed."

"This isn't the best time—" Her voice broke, but she regained her composure. "So don't you dare start in on me
again, Reed. You did more than enough of that last night."

"I dare, lady, because I've watched you dig such a deep
hole for yourself in the past month that you'll never climb

out of it in one piece. I dare," he pronounced angrily, what little restraint he had left fast disappearing, "because you're killing yourself to prove some insane point to the world."

She sat very still, her normally glowing skin so pale it looked almost translucent in the morning light. "And what point is that?"

"That you don't need help from anyone. That you can single-handedly beat the world at its own game. That you don't bleed when someone wounds you. And that you're so self-sufficient you can go it alone, day in and day out. Enough said?" he demanded.

"You're wrong."

"No, Jade. That's the saddest part about this whole mess, because I'm not wrong—not by a long shot."

Devastated, she whispered, "I'm not alone when I'm with you."

"You might as well be." He raked desperate fingers through his hair. His anxiety showed in every tense muscle of his big body. "We both might as well be."

"I don't understand."

"I know," he said harshly. "That's the real irony of all this."

"You're not making any sense. We have an intimate relationship, so how can I be alone?"

"You could tell me the truth once in a while!" he exploded.

She jumped to her feet. "I've never lied to you."

"Not outright," he conceded. "But you've kept things from me—important things about yourself that I deserve to know."

Frustrated and confused, she waved a hand in his direction. "This is the craziest conversation I've ever had with anyone, except of course last night. But that junkie had an excuse because he was higher than a kite on chemicals. You don't.'' She paused for a much-needed gulp of air. "Why are you doing this to me, Reed? What can you hope to gain by throwing me even more off balance than I already am? I'm supposed to give a speech in an hour. I'm already nervous enough.''

"Damn it, woman, you keep proving my point! And you're not giving a speech this morning, Jade. I canceled it. You *are* going to see my doctor at the Scripps Clinic for a thorough exam, and then you're coming back here for some much-needed rest. If you push yourself any harder, you're going to drop in your tracks.''

"If I don't push any harder, I'll fail the children who need the center!" she cried. "And you had no right to cancel that speech. No right at all!''

He ignored her last comment, primarily because he was sick to death of being reminded that he was on the outside looking in as far as their relationship was concerned. "You need a keeper, lady.''

"Well, it certainly won't be you," she announced.

The look he gave her could have pierced steel. "Everyone's failed you, haven't they? So you've turned yourself into a one-woman army determined to succeed at any cost.'' Reed discarded his common sense. "They blew it with you, from the orphanages to the foster homes, and look at what it's done to you. It's distorted your entire perception of the world, and it's got you running in some insane marathon where you're the only competitor.''

She staggered back a few feet, stunned by what he'd just said. "Orphanages?''

He saw her stricken expression and moved toward her. "Don't look at me that way.''

"Foster homes," she breathed in disbelief. "You had me investigated, didn't you? You sneak. You rotten sneak!''

He sensed that any effort at damage control on his part would be useless, but he couldn't stop himself from trying as he approached her. "Jade..."

"Don't touch me." She backed away from his out-stretched hands and collided with the bar between the living room and the kitchen. "Why... why couldn't you have waited until I could tell you myself? We've never—"

"I know we've never," he cut in sharply, "because you haven't trusted me enough to tell me about your past."

She started to slide along the edge of the bar, her intent obvious as she darted a quick glance at the front door. Grabbing her purse from one of the stools next to the bar as she moved, she fought the tears burning her eyes.

Reed paled. "Don't run from me, Jade. Please, don't run. You're the best part of my life, and I won't let anyone take you away from me, not even you."

"What I'm doing at the center is right," she insisted.

"I won't argue the point that your goals make sense. It's your methods that stink. You've neglected the two most essential elements in this happy little equation. You don't trust anyone, and you refuse to share the responsibility."

"But there hasn't been anyone to trust... until you."

He could feel himself breaking apart inside, but he made himself continue. "Of course there hasn't been anyone. The walls around you are so blasted high, it takes a bulldozer to knock them down. I know, because that's about what it took to get anywhere near you. You don't trust anyone, do you? You refuse to reach out. You keep all kinds of secrets. And you've used the one person you could have trusted."

Horrified, she stared at him. "'Used'? What are you talking about?"

He gave her a hard look. "I've got to give you the credit you've earned, Jade. You're not a victim any longer. No way. The little kid with asthma turned into one hot little number between the sheets, didn't she? Kind of like a sexy piranha."

Jade felt sick to her stomach. She also couldn't believe her ears. Bewildered, she didn't even try to muster a defense.

"Seventeen thousand dollars, lady. Maybe that rings a bell," he goaded, his dark eyes narrowed with fury.

"Seventeen thousand dollars?" she echoed, suddenly experiencing a light-headedness that threatened to turn into a complete loss of consciousness.

She turned abruptly, stumbling into the brass floor lamp behind her. It crashed to the floor. She swayed unsteadily, disbelief rising in billowing waves in her mind as she looked wildly from his face to the damaged shade and shattered glass at her feet and then back at him again.

Reed finally regained control of himself. Jade's apparent disorientation triggered a rush of protectiveness, followed swiftly by a glut of self-reproach. He moved toward her, approaching her in the same way he would any wounded animal. Slowly, and ever so cautiously.

Puzzle pieces slipped into place in her mind, providing a sudden clarity of vision. The beach sounds. The train arriving at the Del Mar station. She'd heard those sounds during her nights with Reed, not just as the background sounds of a phone call. Focused on Reed, she hadn't been searching for clues then, because there hadn't been a reason to. Or so she had thought.

She also remembered her admission to her anonymous caller that she didn't have the final installment payment for the renovations. She recalled the oddly muffled sound of his voice. And she felt the keen bite of betrayal when she realized just how much she'd revealed about her past. Hadn't her caller urged her to deal with the isolation of her life? Hadn't he labeled her loneliness a subtle form of abuse? His words had simply been a variation on a theme that Reed had also relentlessly pursued.

"You're the caller," she breathed.

Ruddy color stained his high cheekbones. He tried a bluff, but it was halfhearted at best. "What are you talking about?"

Eyes wide with shock, she said again, "You're the caller. I trusted you...."

He didn't bother to deny the truth, especially since he couldn't conceal any longer the bitterness or the hurt he felt. It erupted with volcanic force. "You trusted a stranger, a voice on the phone. Don't give yourself too much credit, because you took the easy way out."

"Why?" Tears filled her eyes and blurred her vision. She struggled to remain upright, but even that was an ordeal. "Why?" she whimpered a second time.

Reed clenched his fists in frustration. "You've done something to me that no one else in the world has ever done before, Jade, and in the process I've violated my sense of honor, my integrity, everything I hold dear, in order to understand what makes you drive yourself so hard."

"Honor! Integrity!" she shouted. "You don't even know the meaning of the words, so don't be such a self-righteous hypocrite. You just wanted me in your bed, Reed Townsend, although I'll never understand why."

"I guess that makes us even then, since you slept with me to safeguard the center. We're not so different, after all, are we?"

Stunned, she stared at him before her anger kicked in again. "You're insane. Stay away from me and stay out of my life." She pulled herself together by the sheer force of her will, although her voice grew increasingly unstable as she spoke. "You're to be congratulated, you know. You've just given me a refresher course in why I promised myself years ago not to let anyone get too close. All it ever leads to is heartache. Well, thank you very much for the reminder, Mr. Townsend. I am definitely in your debt.'' As each scathing word fell from her lips, she managed a step toward the front door. ''If you need references, I'll be happy to supply them. You're a real expert.''

''I didn't lie to you.''

She hesitated, a part of her desperate to believe him, but she couldn't because she knew the truth now. ''Don't split hairs. You tricked me. It's the same thing in the final analysis.''

Jade turned, crossed the entryway and fumbled for the doorknob. Reed moved quickly, spun her around and trapped her against the heavy oak door with his powerful body.

Fear flared briefly inside her, but she managed to master it. Given the night she'd just survived and the events now taking place, she seriously considered volunteering for time in a rubber room. ''Let me go,'' she ordered.

''Your car's still at the center. I'll drive you.''

''I'll take a cab.'' Unwilling to look at him, she fixed her gaze on the dense mat of tawny hair that covered his wide chest. It was a mistake. A rush of erotic memories assaulted her. She mentally acknowledged the error and closed her eyes.

''Use my phone,'' he countered.

''No!''

''It's a mile to the nearest one.''

''The walk will do me good. I need some air.''

''Don't do this, Jade. Don't leave without at least trying to fix what's wrong between us.'' He lowered his hands to her shoulders.

She looked up in alarm, the pressure of his body holding her firmly in place and setting off a burst of panic inside her.

She reminded herself that she couldn't afford any vulnerability where he was concerned. "I can't and won't take responsibility for what you've done," she insisted stubbornly, clinging to her hurt in the same way that a child clings to a favorite toy in the dark of night.

"Then take responsibility for your own actions." He moved his hands across her shoulders, his touch soothing, considering the thundering alarm within him.

She shivered as he ran his fingertips up the sides of her neck. He stopped when he had her head anchored in his hands and her face tilted up to his gaze.

"My knee works," she said, sudden fury vibrating within her at his less-than-subtle manipulation. "Don't make me use it."

Anger filled him. Reason and compassion, the usual hallmarks of his nature, escaped his mental grasp. He shoved his hips forward, slamming into her and reminding her of his physical prowess with the grinding pressure of his nearly naked anatomy. But his mouth was oddly gentle as he covered her lips.

Jade held herself so still that the pounding of her heart threatened to deafen her. Then she jerked backward without warning, inadvertently striking her head against the door in her haste to get free of him. Stars briefly cascaded behind her eyes. "Damn you."

"You're damning us both," he warned.

He took her mouth a second time, but this kiss was filled with frustration and a small measure of punishment. His lips moved with fierce hurtfulness. He thrust his tongue into her mouth to vanquish any poised protest. And when he felt her lips tremble beneath his, he knew a self-loathing that nearly crippled him.

Jade struggled, as much against herself as against Reed. She loved him, deeply and desperately, but what he'd done was wrong. She twisted free of him and slid unexpectedly to the left.

Reed lifted his hands and stepped back, filled with shame and intensely aware that he'd been a fool in more ways than one.

"That wasn't fair," he finally admitted in a low voice.

She nodded as she stood in the doorway. She felt so weak, as though her legs would buckle under her if she didn't leave soon. "No, it wasn't fair. In fact, none of this has been fair, has it?"

He looked at her, anguish engulfing him and etching grief into the stark lines of his face. "I didn't mean to hurt you."

"You didn't—at least not physically."

"We need to talk," he said, trying to sound calm.

She shook her head as she fiddled nervously with the shoulder strap of her purse. "You've gone too far this time, Reed. I can forgive almost anything, but not this . . . this violation."

Stunned, he protested, "You make it sound as though I just tried to rape you."

She looked at him, sad, defeated, utterly lost. "You did something just as bad. You raped my faith in you."

With that final comment, she turned and walked out of Reed Townsend's home and out of his life. She didn't expect to ever return to either of them.

Limbo. Jade's life began to remind her of being indefinitely suspended in limbo. While she focused all her time and attention on trying to raise the funding needed for the center, she felt out of step with the world in general.

She managed to limit her contact with Reed in the same manner in which he avoided her during the final weeks of construction at the center—by being absent as much of the time as possible. And whenever a chance encounter did occur, they simply looked through each other. If forced to discuss some aspect of the finishing stages of the renovations, they did so in front of as many members of the construction crew as possible.

Despite her resolution to ignore Reed, Jade began to notice the physical changes in him by the end of the first week. His body, strikingly powerful thanks to the nature of his work, looked leaner to her. She wondered if he was getting proper nourishment and then told herself she was a fool to concern herself with his eating habits.

She worried even more as week number one slid into week number two. She noted the tension in Reed's expression because it had cut deep grooves into the skin around his mouth. The man with the suggestive smile no longer smiled at all. Even his eyes looked haunted and empty to her.

She didn't know that he felt similar concerns each time he saw her. Nor did she realize that he rarely got more than two or three uninterrupted hours of sleep at a stretch because he invariably wakened several times each night, his hands reaching for her and finding nothing but his memories.

The continued popularity of the Activity Center with the Southern California media should have pleased her enormously, but the gap in her life caused by Reed's absence left Jade feeling achingly hollow and profoundly incomplete.

She repeatedly cast Reed from her thoughts, although he just as quickly reappeared. She eventually realized that it would take a very long time to stop loving Reed Townsend, but that was precisely what she knew she had to do if she expected to get on with her life. But life without him was empty, a stark black-and-white affair that had once been filled with color and energy and joy.

She mourned the loss of him even as she struggled to understand the reasons for his duplicity. It hurt to think that he might be right. Honesty, ingrained deeply in her personality, forced her to try to weigh his comments against the emotional baggage she'd carried since childhood. To some degree she knew he was right. She didn't trust people. She'd learned to protect herself, simply because it had been her sole route to survival in an indifferent system.

She wondered, too, if she'd lied to herself at the outset of their relationship. She thought she'd gone into his arms and his bed with her eyes open, aware that she needed to regain the ability to reach out, to make herself more accessible to emotions that most people took for granted.

As she sat in her office at the center, paperwork strewn across her desk, Jade closed her eyes and massaged the dull ache at her temples. She missed Reed more than she had ever thought she could miss anyone. He dominated her thoughts. Sadly, he also still consumed her emotions.

"Jade, are you all right?"

She slowly raised her head and opened her eyes. She stared at him, stunned by his presence. "I'm fine," she heard herself answer in what she hoped sounded like a normal voice.

He approached her desk and dropped an envelope in front of her. Then he stepped back so that he was standing in the center of the room.

As she searched his face, Jade realized that his macho manner was conspicuously absent. The dark circles under his eyes implied exhaustion, and she had to bite her tongue to keep from suggesting that he needed more rest than he was allowing himself. The tenseness evident in his strong jaw and in the rigid set of his broad shoulders seemed to declare continued anger over what had happened between them.

Jade felt trapped between worry that he wasn't taking care of himself and a defensiveness rooted so deeply inside her soul that the end result was an inability to verbalize the confusion and sadness she now experienced. She squelched her desire to simply throw herself into his arms and hang on until his anger passed and they could clear the air. Her pride, which kept her from such an impulsive act, seemed a very reluctant ally as she waited for him to say what was on his mind.

"My mother and youngest sister are arranging a Grand Opening reception for the center," he informed her, his manner and his tone brusque. "The crew's volunteered to come in next Saturday and handle any of the uncrating and furniture moving you might need done."

"Why?" she whispered, her surprise apparent.

"They care about the kids," he explained in a tone of voice that implied she'd somehow missed the obvious. "The press will be invited to the reception. Mom and some of her cronies are handling that part of the operation. Knowing my mother, you'll also be tripping over most of San Diego's city fathers and all the local big-money people, once she gets the word out. My sister is a caterer, so she'll handle the food and the decorations."

"Why are you doing this, Reed?" she persisted, clearly taken aback by his generosity. It was the last thing she had expected.

"What happened between us . . ." He cleared his throat, trying to get his emotions in line. "What I did was wrong. I apologize."

Jade wondered if the emotional confusion she felt showed in her face. Fingering the edge of the envelope that Reed had dropped on her desk, she said, "Your apology is enough. There's no need to give a party."

He felt as though she'd just slapped him. Would she never learn that rejection hurt him, too? "There's every need. There's also a condition. I don't want the press to know about my involvement with the center, other than as the contractor for the renovations." On that final note, he turned and strode toward the door.

Jade jumped up from her chair and raced after him, unaware that she held the sealed envelope in her hand. "Reed! Please wait. I'd like to talk to you for a minute, if you have the time."

He felt her hand on his arm. She might as well have branded him with a hot iron. He knew he couldn't be near her for long without giving in to his desire to touch her. He jerked free of her in a wholly self-protective gesture. His wounded pride made him sound cold and hard as he spoke. "I'm a busy man, Jade. You'll have to make it quick."

"The work you and your crew have done on the center is wonderful. I couldn't have asked for a better job." Curious, she couldn't keep herself from asking, "Why don't you want the press to be made aware of your generosity?"

"It's none of their business."

His emphatic tone of voice surprised her. It had been her experience that most people liked to take credit for their charitable contributions. But then, Reed Townsend wasn't like most people. "You feel that strongly about protecting your privacy?"

"Right."

"Then I won't tell anyone."

He nodded, his eyes hungrily scanning her face as he looked down at her, his fingers tense as he fought the need to stroke the curves and hollows of her body one last time.

"Is that all you wanted, Jade?"

She exhaled softly. She knew she'd already put this off long enough, so she forged ahead. "I won't be able to make the final payment on the renovations for at least a month."

His gaze narrowed. He reached out, ignored her gasp of surprise, and seized her wrist. He raised her right hand so that the envelope he'd previously tossed on her desk and that she now clutched like a weapon was positioned at her eye level.

Jade struggled to free herself, too caught up in the turmoil set in motion inside her at his touch to note his grim-faced reaction to her resistance.

"You don't owe Foothills Construction a dime."

"Of course I do."

Reed stiffened. "Your account is paid in full. The proof you need is in this envelope. Use the money from the donations to keep the center's doors open."

She stared at him, the shock she felt evident in her wide eyes as she peered up at him uncertainly.

"Don't look so amazed. I told you during one of our conversations that I'd handle the final payment. I always make a habit of keeping my promises."

"No. You said you'd look into the matter. I didn't think..." Her voice trailed off. She felt the buffeting force of the chemistry that still swirled between them.

"Sometimes it's better not to think. Sometimes, Jade, just letting your feelings guide you gets you a lot farther in the long run."

"Will you be at the reception?" she asked.

"Would you rather I didn't attend?"

She hesitated, unaware that Reed's insides tightened painfully with the stunning force of her apparent eagerness to be rid of him now that the renovations were almost history.

"It's up to you, of course," she finally whispered, her expression reflecting the bleakness of her spirit and her soul.

He reached out in an instinctive gesture, but then forced himself to lower his hand before he made a total fool of himself. "Take care of yourself, Jade. I won't forget you."

He turned and began the long walk down the hallway, his steps slowing only briefly when he heard her final comment.

"I don't forgive easily, Reed, but I'm trying."

Inside the turbulent confines of her mind, a voice shouted, *I need time to understand. Just give me some time to deal with this mess!* Jade, however, remained silent, too distraught to speak as she fought the tears threatening to overcome her.

She lost the battle. Tears slid down her cheeks when he didn't say anything. As the sound of his footsteps faded, she longed for one final, bittersweet taste of the man who possessed her heart.

Ten

After three intense hours of hostessing the Sunday-afternoon reception, chatting with the various attendees and being interviewed by the local TV reporters, Jade slipped away from the crush of guests for a much-needed moment of privacy.

The interior of the Activity Center, which had been decorated with gaily colored balloons and large bouquets of flowers, reminded Jade of a festive garden party. As she watched the interplay between homeless children and their parents and the dignitaries and media people invited to launch the remodeled center, she couldn't stop thinking about Reed.

It had been Reed and his construction crew, Jade knew, who had breathed new life into the run-down warehouse.

She felt a sense of accomplishment as she looked around, but she was aware that while the concept for the center had been hers, the actual execution of the design had taken more than competence and quality workmanship; the center reflected needs understood and met. She sighed heavily and continued to dwell on the man responsible for the realization of her dream.

Instead of erecting a series of closed-in rooms in the ten-thousand-square-foot high-ceilinged center, Reed had worked with the architect and made certain that the children's activity areas flowed together in a harmonious blending of design and practicality.

She studied it all with satisfaction, her gaze drifting from the modest library to the glassed-in tutorial classroom and counseling rooms, then to the indoor volleyball court, a vast play area nearby that could be converted to accommodate a variety of sports and activities, and finally to the "family room," which was an enormous conversation pit littered with child-size beanbag chairs. Her satisfaction, however, was tinged with a hint of melancholy—a feeling she hadn't been able to shake all day.

A flash of bright color halted her survey of the center. The woman was beautiful, so slim and elegant that Jade immediately felt like a dumpy mushroom. Her escort, a tall, broad-shouldered man in a three-piece gray suit, stood just behind her, his back to the crowd. From her vantage point, Jade realized that he was chatting with Mrs. Townsend and her daughter, the caterer.

Jade absently noted the physical compatibility of the couple and wondered who they were. When the man turned to make a comment to the woman and then slide his arm around her waist in a startlingly familiar way, Jade felt her heart stutter to a stop in her chest as she recognized him. Reed.

She wanted to run and hide, but a small child raced toward her, a clutch of balloons in her fist. Kelly, her scraped knee healed and her hair a youthful reproduction of the shoulder-length bob Jade wore, grinned and revealed a small cache of chocolate-chip cookies in her other hand.

Jade dropped to one knee and focused on the little girl, who was now in her temporary custody thanks to the unannounced departure from San Diego, her own children in tow, of Kelly's aunt. The two shared Jade's tiny apartment while they slogged their way, by mutual agreement and with the written authorization provided by Kelly's aunt, through the legal minefield that would hopefully make them mother and daughter in the near future.

They needed each other, as much to replace those they had lost as to fill one another's lives. They also loved each other.

"That man's here," Kelly whispered conspiratorially.

Jade tucked a lock of dark hair behind the child's ear as she tried to steady her frantic heart. "I saw him."

"I like him, even though he yells sometimes."

Jade smiled in spite of the shock reeling through her. Out of the mouths of babes. "He does yell with the best of them, doesn't he?"

Kelly leaned forward, with one arm slung around Jade's neck so that the balloons she held bobbed behind both their heads. "I saw him kiss you one time. Does that mean he might be my dad, since you're gonna be my mom?"

Unprepared for the question, Jade tried to formulate a coherent reply, but words failed her. She sensed Reed's presence even before she looked up to find him towering over her. She lurched to her feet.

"Wanna cookie?" Kelly asked, innocently filling in the conversational gap as Jade and Reed watched each other.

The woman in fuchsia silk smiled down at Kelly. "Why don't we find some punch to go with those cookies, young lady?"

Jade unconsciously tugged Kelly closer, her eyes traveling between Reed and his companion.

"Caroline..." Reed muttered, warning in his voice.

Caroline ignored him and extended her hand. Kelly glanced up at Jade, who reluctantly nodded her permission.

"I won't take her far," Caroline told Jade with a warm smile.

Jade simply nodded again, too bewildered to do anything else. She hated to admit it, but Reed's date seemed very nice.

"Caroline!" Reed said sharply, looking for all the world like a man who had just been pitched stark naked and weaponless into a tank filled with sharks.

The willowy brunette glanced over her shoulder and flashed him a smile that reminded Jade of toothpaste commercials and TV weather girls. "This is your play, big brother, so don't blow it."

Big brother?

Caroline and Kelly headed for the punch bowl while Jade looked questioningly at Reed and grappled with the confusion reflected in her strained features. "She's quite beautiful."

Reed shifted uncomfortably. "She's an airhead!"

She exhaled in a rush. "She's a beautiful airhead, then."

He grinned at that, and some of the tension eased out of him. "Truer words were never spoken."

"So is Kathleen. Beautiful, I mean."

He shrugged, brotherly pride shining through his facade of indifference. "Those two definitely cleaned up in the looks department."

"Your mother holds her own very nicely," Jade noted for the record, her eyes traveling feverishly across his hard-featured face. Nature might have gifted the Townsend women with beauty, but Reed possessed the kind of masculine appeal most men would kill for.

"How are you?"

"Fine, thank you," she answered, though she really felt strangely ill at ease.

"The rumor mill says Kelly's living with you now."

Jade nodded. "Her aunt left her at the homeless shelter about a week ago. Fortunately, she also left a letter placing Kelly in my custody. I've got a lawyer working on the arrangements with the child welfare people." She looked stubborn and determined. "She needs me, and I won't fail her."

Reed wasn't surprised by her decision or by the expression, so fiercely maternal, on her face. He'd already witnessed the link that bound the two together. "She's a sweet kid. You'll be a good parent."

Her mouth twisted wryly. "You actually think I'm capable of doing something other than running the center?"

He muttered a harshly explicit word, seized her by the arm and hustled her down the hallway to her office. Jade gave up any thought of protest when she saw the look on his face.

He propelled her into her office and kicked the door shut. The ceiling, repaired the previous week, no longer snowed cracked plaster. Jade stood in the center of the room, glaring at Reed even as she ground her teeth together.

"How long are you going to keep this up?" he demanded as he tugged his tie loose, yanked it off and then stuffed it into his jacket pocket. He approached her, his eyes boring holes into her flesh and lighting brushfires inside her as he released the two top buttons of his shirt.

"I don't know what you're talking about."

"Don't you?"

"No, I don't!"

"This is useless. I don't even know why I thought I could have a rational conversation with you." He turned abruptly and walked to the door, his footsteps making sharp exclamation marks on the wood floor.

"Can't we at least be friends?" Jade asked impulsively. She didn't want this to be their last time together.

He hesitated, his hand poised over the doorknob. "It's not enough." He pivoted slowly, his eyes the darkest navy blue, his expression brooding. "It's just not enough."

Anger, frustration and hope left her as she sighed quietly. "I was afraid you'd feel that way."

"I've been your lover, and I've tasted your passion, lady. I want it again, and I won't settle for less. You'll be in my bed, or you won't be in my life."

Shock rattled through her, jarring her, robbing her of her composure. Unable to look Reed in the eye, she walked to the single window in her office, unaware that he'd made it halfway across the room before he managed to stop himself.

Jade didn't really see the alley, but she knew the trash cans lodged there were upright now and corralled behind a chain link fence. The choice was hers, she realized. One conciliatory word, less single-minded defiance, more sharing, and she would have her lover back.

But would that be enough? she wondered. After two weeks in emotional limbo, could she accept the uncertainty inherent in being involved with Reed without a real commitment? She let the silence between them drag on, aware that she also had to factor Kelly into this complex equation.

Her silence gnawed on his nerves. "Offering me friendship is like offering a thirsty man a bucket of salt. I need more, Jade." His voice was quiet, even gentle, and sounded so much the way the caller always had.

She gripped the windowsill, thrown off balance by that subdued gentleness and the rush of memories it provoked. She could feel herself turning inward, a protective action meant to block out the overwhelming sense of loss she experienced each time she thought about Reed Townsend.

But instead of the relief she sought, she felt the walls in her mind—walls that had always been a part of her self-protective nature—begin to break apart. And she remembered...she finally remembered with remarkable clarity the content, the real essence, of their shared confidences. They had both been honest and achingly vulnerable, she realized, especially him.

She suddenly felt betrayed, but not by Reed. Betrayed, instead, by her own emotional upset and the lack, on her part, of any real understanding of the significance of their conversations once she'd discovered his dual identity.

Now, neither one had the safety of anonymity to protect them. The caller—Reed—had been heartbreakingly candid. Her hurt over their breakup, her perception of his duplicity, the center and Kelly's entrance into her life—all had prevented her from viewing their relationship from every angle during the past few weeks. Instead, she'd selfishly looked at Reed from one damning perspective.

"Oh, God!" she gasped suddenly. "Dear God! How could I have forgotten?"

Jade whirled around to face him. She saw his vulnerability, no longer hidden beneath a macho demeanor that suited only one aspect of his life. She saw the hunger in his eyes, no longer concealed by sarcasm or humor. She thought of the boy who had been beaten and abused, but who had survived to become a man of sensitivity and courage.

And she thought about the two men she'd grown to love, the two men she had once thought would be perfect if spliced together to form one complete man. The combination of compassion and strength would be devastating. Reed, in fact, was devastating.

She also recalled the condition of privacy demanded by the caller and finally understood the real reason for that one requirement. Reed's pride—understandable, given his childhood experiences—necessitated that privacy. She knew now that he had no real desire to hurt her, use her or even trick her.

Reed saw it all, too. He saw his past in Jade's eyes. "I don't want your pity."

She took a hesitant step forward. "I don't pity you, Reed. I pity myself. I've been so caught up in my own concerns that I haven't taken an honest look at what happened between us until now."

He shoved blunt-tipped fingers through his short, cropped hair, the gesture a sign of both his agitation and his need for fairness. "Don't beat yourself up. I haven't been all that easy on you, and I did deceive you."

She nodded, her expression serious. "You did, but I'm beginning to understand why."

"Then maybe you'll see your way clear to listening to what I'm about to say."

"Of course, I'll listen," she insisted, her heart near to bursting with the love she felt for him.

He appeared to fight some brief inner battle that ended with him clenching his fists at his sides before he spoke. Tapping into a somewhat shallow well of hope, he admitted, "I've told myself a thousand times that I'm not the kind of man you deserve to have in your life. You're well educated, and I barely made it out of high school. You've got more class than any woman I've ever known. I may have money, but I'll never have any real class. You deserve some guy who'll treat you like a queen, Jade, but I'm not the type to put a woman on a pedestal. I need a partner. In return, I'm willing to be a full partner in her life, too.''

Jade took another step in his direction, hoping, praying that he wanted her as much as she wanted him. She didn't care what she had to do. She wasn't going to lose him. ''Reed—''

''Let me finish. This is hard enough as it is.''

She nodded, although she kept inching forward. The man was going to drive her crazy. He always had. She suspected that he always would.

''I'm no great prize, Jade, but my needs are pretty basic and my tastes are simple. I know what I like and I go after it full throttle. That's just my way. I know how you feel about the center. You probably even think I want you to bow out of the place, but I don't. I just want you to let me help you shoulder all the responsibility you've taken on. I'll help you, if you'll let me. But you have to tell me straight out what you need for these kids, because I don't read minds. If you want, we can get married right away. That way you and Kelly will have the right kind of home, not some damn box that looks like a motel room.''

She couldn't take any more of this. ''Reed, stop talking!''

He paled and turned away from her without another word. As he headed for the door, he told himself that he didn't need a hammer thrown at his head to remind him that he could bleed. He also told himself that he was a fool for hoping that Jade might consider him potential husband and father material.

She darted around in front of him before he could jerk open the door and walk out of her life once and for all. Peering up at him, her small figure the sole barrier between Reed and the closed door, she smiled. He frowned warily when he saw the satisfied look on her face.

Aware of the risk she was about to take, Jade asked softly, "Since you seem determined to take on a ready-made family, do you think you could tell me how you really feel about me?"

"I've been trying to tell you how I feel!" he barked.

"What do you want from me, Reed?"

"I want you."

"Then why don't you just say the words?"

"I love you, damn it!"

She launched herself into his arms, relief and joy rocketing through her. "Without the 'damn it' part, please."

He lowered his voice, his tone rueful as he said, "I love you, Jade Howell. I love you more than my life."

Looping her arms around his neck, she grinned. "Again please."

He gave her one of those scintillating, guaranteed-to-scorch-your-soul smiles of his that made Jade feel as though she was about to melt all over him.

"I love you, sweet lady."

He lowered his head then and took her lips. Several minutes later, Jade sighed shakily as Reed held her in his arms. Something nagged at her, once she floated back down to earth. "What's all that stuff about you not being any great prize?"

He looked away from her probing gaze, but he kept a secure hold on her when she tried to wriggle free. "You've probably got a couple of hundred people wondering if you've been stolen by little green men from Mars. We can talk later."

She shook her head, the stubborn angle of her chin a certain sign that she wasn't budging until she'd had her say. "It's your turn to listen, Reed Townsend, and I'm not going anywhere until you do."

"So, spit it out, lady," he muttered.

She reached up and placed her hands on his cheeks, her touch as gentle as the expression filtering into her eyes. "You seem to have some crazy idea that I have a laundry list of requirements regarding the kind of man I'll let myself love, but the truth is that I've loved you from the very start. I fought the feelings, because I was frightened of caring and I was even more frightened of being abandoned if I admitted that I loved you."

She tugged him forward so that she could press a butterfly-soft kiss on his lips. "You're everything I've ever wanted in a man, Reed Townsend. And even though you've got the temperament of exploding dynamite, I think you are the most honorable, the brightest, the most decent and loving man I've ever known. You have the kind of courage and strength that I want our children to have. I'm proud to love you, and I'm even prouder that you love me."

"You're something else, sweet lady."

A knock sounded on the door, reminding them both of the two hundred assorted guests that Jade had abandoned. Reed gave her a quick kiss and yanked open the door. His mother, two sisters and Kelly looked expectantly at the couple.

"Kathleen, do you think you're up to planning a wedding and reception in under two weeks?" Reed finally asked after a sixty-second staring contest.

"Two weeks?" all five females chorused.

Shocked, Jade squeezed Reed's hand until her own fingers went numb. "Is that your idea of a romantic proposal?"

He nodded and simply waited. The expression on his face didn't provide anyone with a clue to his thoughts.

"In that case," she said, "I accept."

The four females standing on the other side of the threshold to Jade's office cheered, and the sound still echoed down the hallway long after Reed kicked the door shut and proceeded to demonstrate to his prospective bride the wisdom of her acceptance of his marriage proposal.

*   *   *   *   *

 **Diamond Jubilee Collection**

It's our 10th Anniversary... and *you* get a present!

This collection of early Silhouette Romances features novels written by three of your favorite authors:

ANN MAJOR—*Wild Lady*
ANNETTE BROADRICK—*Circumstantial Evidence*
DIXIE BROWNING—*Island on the Hill*

* These Silhouette Romance titles were first published in the early 1980s and have not been available since!

* Beautiful Collector's Edition bound in antique green simulated leather to last a lifetime!

* Embossed in gold on the cover and spine!

This special collection will not be sold in retail stores and is only available through this exclusive offer.
Look for details in all Silhouette series published in June, July and August.

Take 4 bestselling love stories FREE

Plus get a FREE surprise gift!

COMING SOON...

For years Harlequin and Silhouette novels have been taking readers places—but only in their imaginations.

This fall look for PASSPORT TO ROMANCE, a promotion that could take you around the corner or around the world!

Watch for it in September!

★